"Okay. We're alone. Why did you come looking for me?"

"I thought that was obvious."

How could Ida have forgotten the intensity of that brooding stare? Cesare's eyes bored into hers as if seeking out misdemeanors or weaknesses.

But she'd done him no wrong. She didn't owe him anything and refused to be cowed by that flinty gaze. Ida shoved her hands deep in her raincoat's pockets and raised her eyebrows.

"It's been a long day, Cesare. I'm not in the mood for guessing games. Just tell me. What do you want?"

He crossed the space between them in a couple of deceptively easy strides. Deceptive because his expression told her it was the prowl of a predator.

"To sort out our divorce, of course."

"We're still married?"

Growing up near the beach, **Annie West** spent lots of time observing tall, burnished lifeguards—early research! Now she spends her days fantasizing about gorgeous men and their love lives. Annie has been a reader all her life. She also loves travel, long walks, good company and great food. You can contact her at annie@annie-west.com or via PO Box 1041, Warners Bay, NSW 2282, Australia.

Books by Annie West

Harlequin Presents

The Sheikh's Marriage Proclamation
A Consequence Made in Greece
The Innocent's Protector in Paradise
One Night with Her Forgotten Husband
The Desert King Meets His Match

Royal Scandals

Pregnant with His Majesty's Heir
Claiming His Virgin Princess

Visit the Author Profile page
at Harlequin.com for more titles.

Annie West

RECLAIMING HIS
RUNAWAY CINDERELLA

HARLEQUIN®
PRESENTS™

Recycling programs
for this product may
not exist in your area.

ISBN-13: 978-1-335-58389-5

Reclaiming His Runaway Cinderella

Harlequin Enterprises ULC
22 Adelaide St. West, 41st Floor
Toronto, Ontario M5H 4E3, Canada
www.Harlequin.com

Printed in U.S.A.

RECLAIMING HIS RUNAWAY CINDERELLA

I'm delighted and amazed to say that this is my 50th book for Harlequin! I hope you enjoy reading it as much as I had fun writing it. I'd never have reached fifty books without lots of help, encouragement and understanding from my family, who are all fabulous and inspiring; my dear writer friends (you know who you are), who listen and chivy, problem-solve and celebrate; my excellent editor; and you lovely readers who continue to pick up my books and share the worlds I create.

Thank you all for making this career and all these stories possible!

CHAPTER ONE

THE FAMILIAR MUSIC began and behind him Cesare heard a hush descend on the packed church. Not a complete silence, for even over the triumphant swell of music came the sound of hundreds of whispers and the rustle of designer dresses as people turned towards the entrance.

Cesare waited, eyes straight ahead, as if taking in the gilded pomp of the renaissance interior.

But his thoughts were elsewhere. On the events which had culminated in today's ceremony. The circumstances, some predictable, others unforeseen, all compelling. All pushing him to this moment.

A collective sigh gathered behind him, and it felt as if the air in the vast space thickened. The scent from the elaborate floral arrangements grew more intense and the bone-white candles flickered in their silver candelabras.

The priest flicked him a look and Cesare knew it was time to turn.

Finally he swung around, his eyes going unerringly to the figure halfway up the aisle.

Now he understood the sighs.

Ida Montrose looked ethereal, floating down the aisle in a long, gauzy dress that looked held together by wisps of lace.

There was lace too on the veil that covered her

face and draped her shoulders. But through it he saw the golden-red gleam of her hair and the huge pools of her eyes.

He hadn't meant to, but he couldn't stop his gaze dropping. Pausing at the sweet swell of her breasts, barely covered by white lace, down to a waist so narrow his fingers twitched at the thought of spanning it.

The dress clung to her neat hips then fell in folds of transparent fabric and lace that made her look like a cross between a flower fairy and a lingerie model.

Cesare's body responded accordingly. With a thudding pulse of heat that plunged from his chest to his suddenly aching groin.

His lungs stopped as he imagined his hands on her. Big hands ruthlessly parting those insubstantial layers to reveal satiny skin. Eager hands palming her pale body and preparing her for his possession.

Heat shot through him like flames through a petrol-soaked bonfire. Moisture beaded his hairline and nape while a jab of pain told him he was clenching his jaw in the effort of control.

This wouldn't do. He had a solemn ceremony to get through under the watchful gaze of Europe's oldest families and monied elite.

He yanked his gaze away from his bride to the man walking down the aisle beside her. White-haired, wearing a satisfied grin. Fausto Calogero.

It might be years since the man had frequented

Rome, but he nodded and smiled as if he knew half the high-born guests, his chest thrust out in pride.

Cesare took a slow breath and schooled his features.

He didn't fool himself that after today he'd be able to ignore the man. But as of today, things would change. Cesare would make sure of that.

The pair paused at the bottom of the steps and Cesare's attention snapped back to his bride-to-be. She was so close he saw the puff of movement as her breath stirred the veil, and the way the pure white lilies and orange blossom trembled in her hands.

But her chin was high, and he felt her gaze on him.

She wanted this wedding and so did he.

Cesare let his expression ease into a smile of pure anticipation.

Soon he'd have exactly what he wanted.

Ida should be exhausted.

She'd barely slept the night before and today's formalities had gone on for ever.

First, she'd had to run the gauntlet of her grandfather's eagle-eyed inspection. He'd paid for her to be turned out in style and that gave him the right to bark orders at the coterie of dressers, make-up artists, hairstylists and even the poor florists who'd attended her.

It hadn't occurred to Ida to suggest how *she'd* like to look on her wedding day. Or object that the flesh- coloured backing in her diaphanous gown made her look like a raunchy parody of the virginal bride her grandfather had intended.

You didn't argue with Fausto Calogero.

Then there'd been the wedding in one of Rome's most venerated churches, filled to standing with well-heeled, well-connected people she didn't know.

Finally had come the reception. Hours of polite conversation, exquisite food that she'd been too keyed-up to eat and vintage wines she'd never heard of, but which had made her grandfather nod approvingly.

There'd been dancing till her feet ached and photographs till her face ached and stares from people who didn't bother to conceal surprise or dismay that Cesare Brunetti had married *her*.

Yet Ida was too wired to think of sleep.

Because she was in the opulent prestige suite of Rome's most famous and expensive private hotel. And her husband was in the next room. *Waiting for her.*

Ida shivered. Not with cold. And only with a little trepidation.

No, it was excitement that rushed through her like a scouring tide. Anticipation that made her skin tingle and her blood pump faster.

She looked in the mirror and saw the hard points of her nipples jutting against the midnight-blue silk of her new nightie. Her hands shook as she smoothed the whisper-thin fabric from her hips to her thighs.

The sensation was unfamiliar, and not simply because she'd never worn a sexy silk nightdress before. The brush of fabric under her palms made her think of *his* hands on her. Would they be slow and easy or urgent and needy? Her breath quickened, intensifying the unfamiliar, heavy feeling low in her body, like a throbbing ache.

Ida met her eyes in the mirror, and they told the same tale. They were wide and bright, almost feverish with anticipation.

Had she done right to take her hair down? It rippled around her shoulders and even that felt like a caress.

Would Cesare know, just by looking, how she felt?

She frowned and reached for the dark blue silk robe, slipping her arms into it and tying it at her waist. Now her puckered nipples weren't so obvious.

Ida shook her head. What did it matter? As soon as Cesare took her to bed he'd realise how eager she was.

She hoped her inexperience wouldn't mar their first night together. Cesare, scion of an ancient, aristocratic family, blessed with stunning good looks, money, magnetism and an aura of power, could have any woman he wanted. No doubt he'd had plenty, even if he kept his romantic conquests private.

It still astounded her that he wanted *her*.

She wasn't naïve enough to think he loved her. They'd met because he and her grandfather had become business associates and, as he'd explained, he needed a wife.

But he'd chosen *her*. Ida Montrose.

Not one of the uber-sophisticated socialites who'd looked daggers at her during the reception. Not the glamorous princess who'd flown in for the wedding and looked as if she'd like to gobble Cesare up.

To Cesare Ida was convenient. But there was more to it. There was an affinity between them, and Ida *knew* they could build on that to make a success of this marriage.

She'd felt the powerful connection in the way he looked at her. In those rare, devastating smiles. The way he actually listened when she spoke.

There'd even been times, when her grandfather laid down the law about something, when Cesare had caught her eye and she'd felt their connection and shared understanding. She'd felt the impatience he was too well-bred to show, the riposte he was too polite to make.

Cesare…her husband…wasn't cowed by her grandfather. That, above all else, gave her hope for the future and courage to go through with this. He'd chosen her as his bride because he *wanted* her.

As she wanted him.

Now he was hers.

She was nineteen and all her dormant female longings had rushed to the surface the moment she met him.

Life hadn't given her opportunities to date or simply get to know many men. But she was ready to make up for that. Not because she was desperate for a man. That hadn't been a priority. It was *Cesare* who made her want to explore the sensual delights she knew he'd share with her.

Ida looked down at the rings weighting her left hand. The gold wedding band and the engagement ring with its enormous square-cut diamond solitaire.

She'd work hard at this marriage. She could imagine the pair of them, years from now, easy in each other's company but sharing those glowing, loving looks she still remembered seeing her parents share.

Thinking about that lit a tiny spark of hope deep inside where for so long she'd felt cold and unwanted. Orphaned at eight, she still missed her parents' love.

Her chin firmed and she stood straighter. She slipped off her robe and put it neatly on a nearby chair. Then she breathed deeply and reached for the gilded door handle.

Cesare was in the luxurious sitting room. Not ensconced on a sofa, waiting for her, but on the phone, looking out over the rooftops of Rome.

The sound of his native Italian in that rich voice made her think of dark, molten chocolate and she licked her lips, wondering how he'd taste. That peck in the church had been too quick.

A quiver of arousal ran down her spine and she pressed suddenly clammy hands to her thighs.

Maybe she should have worn the robe after all.

For he was still fully dressed, right down to the lovingly tailored formal black jacket that clung to his wide shoulders and tapering back.

She'd never seen Cesare in moulded-to-the-skin jeans or clinging polo shirts, yet she knew that beneath his urbane exterior was a virile man. He oozed masculinity just as he radiated confidence. Without the latter her grandfather would have steamrollered him as he did everyone else.

Ida's gaze dropped to Cesare's long legs, remembering the way his hard thighs had brushed hers when they danced at the reception. She'd seen heat shimmer in his gaze too.

She might be inexperienced, but she wasn't totally naïve. It had been a look of sensual promise and she couldn't wait for him to deliver.

Ida moved closer, bare feet silent on the thick carpet, enjoying the unaccustomed luxury of watching Cesare unobserved.

He swung around, eyes widening for a second, and satisfaction punched low in her abdomen. He'd sensed her approach. And he hadn't been able to hide his response.

She breathed out, relieved, realising he liked what he saw. She'd aimed for sophisticated and sexy with this nightgown that skimmed rather than hugged her figure. Yet despite the fact it covered her from breastbone to knee, she'd never been so naked before anyone.

Cesare ended the call and pocketed his phone,

then shoved his hands in his trouser pockets, surveying her with a stern look that made her smile falter on her lips.

'Ida.'

Just that. Yet the way his voice deepened to a low, unfamiliar rumble tickled her senses. Surely that was a good sign?

But he made no move towards her. Nor did he make any move to undress. He hadn't even undone his bow tie.

She swallowed. Was that something she should offer to do? Her fingertips tingled at the thought of touching him. The prospect of peeling back that snowy shirt to reveal his powerful chest jammed her breath in her lungs.

Gathering her courage, she walked closer, feeling the weight of his gaze with every step.

Did he like what he saw? She was suddenly conscious of how ordinary she was. Her curves weren't bounteous, her height on the small side.

Mentally she shrugged off her doubts. She'd had a lifetime of her grandfather finding fault. She was determined to start her new life without that baggage.

The future was about her and Cesare. That trounced the flutter of nerves in her abdomen and she smiled.

She'd never been so happy.

She stopped before him, and Cesare felt winded. Her incandescent smile reminded him of the rising sun spilling its golden rays over his beloved Tuscan countryside.

Remarkably he felt it too, like a rush of flame igniting in his belly and shooting along his veins. Heat seared his lungs and groin as he looked into her upturned face.

Everything else vanished. The all-important plans that had to be implemented straight away if he was to achieve his goals. Thoughts of Calogero's stranglehold on Cesare's business, and by extension his life, ebbed from his brain as he basked in that dazzling smile and lost himself in Ida's mesmerising pale green eyes.

She might be Calogero's granddaughter, but she had the face of a Botticelli angel and the form of a young Venus. Rose-gold hair falling in waves around pale shoulders. A rosebud mouth. Slender curves and an aura almost of innocence that even now intrigued him.

Innocence!

That dragged him back to reality.

She couldn't be anything like innocent. Not when she'd been a vital part of the old man's scheme. She was the one who had joined the ancient and proud Brunetti family. As her grandfather's heir and now as Cesare's wife, she'd benefited from Calogero's manipulative schemes.

Cesare spun on his heel and strode to the antique sideboard.

'I'm having a drink. Do you want one?'

Silence for a second. Then an unexpectedly husky voice made his belly clamp tight. 'Thank you. I'll have what you're having.'

Her voice was pure sexual invitation. That raspy whisper belonged to a lounge singer in some smoky bar, all decadent invitation and sultry innuendo.

Cesare swallowed, annoyed to find his pulse racing and his collar too tight. As if he'd never had a woman before. As if he were the nineteen-year-old and she twenty-seven.

As if he didn't know about grasping women.

Or the dangers of letting lust conquer common sense.

Yet, to his amazement, Cesare was in half a mind to dispense with the preliminaries and take her now, hard and fast, right where she stood. Or maybe against the window with the lights of Rome at her back where anyone looking up from the piazza could see him debauching her.

The turbulent emotions he'd held in harness all day were close to detonation point.

That realisation steadied his hand as he poured them both a glass of Sangiovese. Cesare hadn't come this far to bend at the first provocation. No matter how tempting.

He'd learned the dangers of losing control. If his dead father had done the same, the family wouldn't be in this predicament.

He swung around, a glass in each hand, to find her still standing in the centre of the room. Did she

know the overhead light turned her hair to glorious
fire? Or that it revealed her pebbled nipples beneath
that shimmering slip of nothing?

Undoubtedly. Ida was an expert at managing her
appearance. Demure dresses in pastel shades before
their wedding, emphasising her youth and apparent
innocence. And today's bridal dress, a mix of virgin
and vamp designed to mess with his head.

Cesare passed her a glass, ignoring the frisson of
sensation when their fingers touched. He raised his
glass and took a sip, savouring the wine. Its familiar-
ity steadied him. It was from the family vineyard, a
reminder of things he'd once taken for granted that
were under threat.

Not for much longer, if his plans succeeded.

'Are you coming to bed soon?'

Her soft voice was pure temptation. She looked at
him with big eyes and he wondered how often she'd
used that look to get what she wanted.

But he, Cesare Brunetti, was not at her beck and
call.

'No. I have work to do.'

Her eyebrows wrinkled into a frown. To his annoyance that only made her look cute as well as
sexy. He felt a growl of vexation build at the back
of his throat.

'But it's our wedding night!'

'And?'

He shouldn't enjoy her look of dismay quite so
much. But after the stresses of the past months, it

was one tiny pleasure to give in, just a little, to his white-hot anger. She and her grandfather thought they could yank his chain and have him obey like a whipped dog. He'd had no choice about this marriage but, no matter what the temptation, *he* controlled his sex life.

Cesare took another sip of wine, savouring the rich flavour. That was one success at least. Even if the rest of his plans failed, today he'd secured the vineyard and the jobs of all the workers there. As for the rest of the Brunetti holdings—

'And…don't you want…?'

She shook her head as if too shy to speak plainly. The idea would have amused him if he weren't fed up with pretence.

'Don't I want sex, do you mean?'

Cesare let his gaze travel deliberately down her slender body. He reached her bare feet with their pale pink painted toenails, then trailed his stare back to her face. Her cheeks were flushed and her neck blotchy with heat.

So, she wasn't quite as poised as she appeared.

'I like sex,' he said slowly. 'But I have my standards.'

'Sorry?'

She flinched and a few drops of wine spattered across the gleaming silk she wore.

Cesare thought of what lay beneath the fabric and paused.

Because he *did* want her.

He'd felt the tug of arousal the first day old man
Calogero had led her in to meet him, looking like
some wide-eyed innocent. He'd felt it again and
again at every meeting. Never more so than today
when she'd become his in the eyes of the world.

Some primal part of him wanted nothing more
than to claim her physically, forgetting the debacle
of the last six months as he lost himself inside her.

He resented that she made him so desperate.
Which was why he would not, *could* not, give in
to that need.

'I don't understand.'

He took in the uptilt of her jaw and the way her
mouth flattened and registered that she *still* looked
too delectable. What would it take to eradicate the
weakness he felt around her?

'Then let me make it absolutely clear.'

He paused, watching her breasts hitch with her
indrawn breath, feeling an answering ache in his
groin. In the past there'd been no need for sexual
abstinence and Cesare had enjoyed his lovers, but
a man had his pride.

'I have no interest in bedding a woman like you.
A protégé of that twisted criminal who's damaged
not just my family but plenty of innocents besides.
I wouldn't touch you if you were the last woman
in Italy.'

CHAPTER TWO

HE MEANT IT. He really meant it.

Stunned, Ida felt his words stab into soft flesh.

She gripped the wine glass so hard it was a wonder it didn't shatter. Wine slopped over the brim onto her hand, but she didn't look down. She couldn't break Cesare's gaze. It felt as if she was locked into the high beam of that laser-like stare.

Yet it seemed imperative that she keep hold of the glass, so she wrapped her left hand around the frozen knuckles of her right, trying to steady it.

Because it gave her something to think about other than the hatred in her husband's dark brown eyes.

Before this she'd thought his eyes velvety and warm, a welcome contrast to the mean glitter of her grandfather's furious stare. Now Cesare's eyes were so cold she felt ice crackle along her bones and frost her skin. He looked pitiless.

'But I—'

'Don't bother making excuses. It doesn't matter.'

'Of course it matters. We're *married*!'

This was some terrible mistake. They'd promised to build a future together, to—

'Exactly. You got what you wanted. A high-profile husband and the cachet of an aristocratic family name to open doors for your social aspirations.'

Ida shook her head, hair swirling wildly around her face. How could he think that? What about the times, albeit brief, when they'd talked and she'd thought that they shared the beginnings of a real connection?

But when she opened her mouth to object he spoke over her.

'Your grandfather got what he wanted, didn't he? All those years scheming and cheating to bring down the family he hated. To manipulate us and strike a fatal blow that gives him control over our company and us.'

Cesare paused, chest heaving, and Ida felt the fury throb through him. It clogged the air between them.

If she could have moved away she would. Ida knew how dangerous a truly irate man could be. Beneath her, one ankle buckled as if that old injury had resurfaced, and it took everything she had to stand tall. The only parts of her that moved were her thundering heart and shaking hands.

She wouldn't cower. Yet she had a horrible, dizzy feeling, as if the walls pushed in and she might collapse. Cesare made it sound like her grandfather had orchestrated their marriage as part of some vengeful scheme. But that couldn't be true. Her grandfather *was* thrilled about the wedding, and he used people for his own ends, but Cesare was wealthy and powerful. He made his own choices.

'But he wanted more, didn't he?' Cesare snarled.

'It wasn't enough just to ruin the family enterprises, he wanted what he'd never had. A chance to lord it over us. Acceptance in polite society. Entry to the world that draws the line at gangsters, blackmailers and murderers.'

Her gasp was loud in the thick silence.

With an effort Ida finally managed to swallow, though it felt like her throat closed around shards of glass.

'You're exaggerating.'

Her grandfather was awful. No one knew that better than her. But a murderer?

'Which part of the truth don't you like, Ida? That I don't want you in my bed, or that I won't play your grandfather's games and pretend he's honest and respectable?'

She wasn't going to beg for Cesare in her bed.

'I know he's not honest.' He was ruthless and vicious, but he wasn't a murderer. Was he? She frowned. 'But he's not a murderer. And you're mistaken about me.'

'Am I?' Cesare put his glass down and folded his arms. The movement accentuated his height and the breadth of his chest as if he deliberately tried to intimidate her. 'You mean he forced you into this marriage?'

Ida sucked in much-needed air then finally scraped out a response. 'No, he didn't force me.'

Because she'd seen marriage to Cesare as her chance to escape. She'd believed they could build something special together. Because she wanted him and thought he wanted her.

More fool her!

The stabbing pain was worse now, carving through her middle.

She looked into that handsome, severe face, noting the sneering curl to Cesare's sculped mouth and the flare of chiselled nostrils, as if he detected a foul smell. And those eyes... There was no mistaking that expression for anything but distaste.

Suddenly Ida felt ashamed of the hopes and plans she'd woven around this man. Of the tenderness she'd harboured and the budding attraction she'd felt.

More than budding. She had a full-blown crush on the man.

Correction. She'd *had* one. It wouldn't survive this, for which she was thankful. Imagine pining for a man who looked at you like you were dirt under his polished shoe!

She'd been sucked in by what she realised now had been polite manners and his determination not to reveal his true feelings until the deed was done and they were married.

Because you were naïve.

Because he was the first man since your dad to be gentle and kind to you.

Because you're a late bloomer and you've never had a chance for romance.

'You admit you married me of your own free will?'

Fury spiked and she welcomed it. It was better than the devastating feeling that everything inside her was collapsing into an aching void.

'Are you hard of hearing, Cesare?'

He blinked and she saw his pulse throb, quick and hard in his jaw. He hadn't expected her to challenge him.

A lifetime's training told her she shouldn't have spoken so. Provoking or even inadvertently annoying a man who was bigger and stronger than you was a huge mistake. But as she tensed, ready for his response, she saw him draw a deep breath and lower his shoulders, as if seeking calm.

Ida stared. The way Cesare reined in his anger when she argued back told her he *was* completely different to her grandfather. He was irate but instinct told her he'd use only words as his weapons.

Stupid to feel a burst of admiration at the knowledge.

'So you admit you married by choice. You were greedy for what I had and you didn't. The aristocratic title and connections. And the chance to be a spy for your grandfather in the enemy camp. He thinks he has the upper hand now, but he'll want to know I'm toeing the line at all times, so everything goes just as he wants.'

Ida considered denying it. But that would leave

her needing to explain why she *had* agreed to marry a man she barely knew.

She felt like she'd shrivel up and die if Cesare realised she'd acted on sheer romantic dreams and a desperation to escape.

He'd scoff at the first. As for the second, he thought her in cahoots with her grandfather. He'd never believe her protestations. Even if by some miracle he eventually did, he'd never understand.

For despite his talk of her grandfather having the upper hand, Cesare was one of the strongest, most capable and determined people she'd met. He radiated power and self-control. It was one of the first things she'd noticed about him. Along with his looks and charisma. And she'd read about his formidable business acumen, even though he wasn't yet thirty.

He wouldn't understand what it was like to be helpless. How desperate you could be. How much you'd dare.

'Why did *you* marry *me*, Cesare?'

At last she managed to unfreeze her muscles and took a couple of steps to a side table, where she put down the glass. She hoped she looked nonchalant though she felt like a marionette, pulled on jerky strings.

Cesare's stare, less ferocious but no less daunting, had her folding her arms tight around her middle. How she wished she'd worn that robe. Or something much more substantial than silk and naked skin.

Every time she moved, the shift of thin material across bare flesh made her skin prickle.

'You're going to play the innocent?'

Ida shrugged. What could she say that he'd believe? 'It's a simple question.'

'This is pointless.' He lifted his glass and took a long swallow as if he needed something to ease his mood.

'You owe me more than insults.' Ida watched him lower his glass, surprise on his features. 'I *married* you today. So you can oblige me by explaining your insinuations.'

Her tone was frosty. It would take years of practice to achieve Cesare's glacial disdain or her grandfather's venomous fury, but it felt good not to leash her feelings as she'd done for so long.

She lifted her chin and ignored the hurried thump of her heart against her breast, warning her to be careful. She'd spent most of her life being careful and look where it had got her.

'Are you going to explain or are you going to drink yourself into a stupor because you're in a bad mood?'

Ida felt her eyes widen as the words escaped. She'd never dared speak like that in her life. But Cesare didn't seem shocked. He merely raised his eyebrows and, holding her gaze, lifted the crystal wine glass to his lips and drank deeply.

It was the strangest feeling, staring back at those

dark eyes. Noticing too the way his throat muscles worked.

It felt…intimate. His glittering stare made her hot and edgy. Aware of him at an elemental level as tension corkscrewed low in her body.

Ida blushed. That wasn't just challenging but also sexual. She felt it even though she couldn't explain how she knew it.

Cesare was toying with her. She spun on her heel, ready to leave, when he spoke.

'You know what your grandfather is. You live with him.'

'Actually, I don't. Not usually.'

He frowned. Maybe her grandfather had painted a picture of them as a close-knit family. It was the sort of thing he'd do if it suited him.

'I'm no apologist for him, but this is the first I've heard about blackmail or murder.'

Cesare stared at her for a long moment then gestured to the sofas. 'Let's sit.'

'I'd rather stand.'

This wasn't going to be a cosy chat. It took all her strength to hear him out, pretending she didn't care that he despised her or that she felt defenceless in nothing but navy silk. But she had to know it all.

Cesare scowled. Because he felt guilty over his accusations? More likely he wasn't used to a woman saying no to him.

Cesare Brunetti had the looks and charisma to make women say yes.

Ida raised her eyebrows, pretending to a calm she didn't feel. 'You were going to explain.'

'It's straightforward enough. Fausto Calogero hated my grandfather and vowed revenge on him and my family. Now he's taking that revenge.'

'Why? What did your family do?'

Cesare stiffened, his cheeks hollowing in an expression of pure hauteur. 'Nothing. Except look after the girl your grandfather attacked and call the police.'

'He attacked a girl?'

Ida rubbed her hands up her bare arms as the chill inside her turned arctic.

'He claimed she wanted him but then changed her mind. But she was the one with the black eye. He would have raped her if *my* grandfather hadn't heard her screams. That was when Fausto left Italy, before the authorities could arrest him. He blamed my grandfather, who was from a respected family, for turning the town against him.'

Ida swallowed the sour taste on her tongue. It shouldn't surprise her. It *didn't* surprise her. Yet she felt ashamed. As if her grandfather's crimes tainted her.

Was it true that her marriage was part of a scheme for vengeance? She'd heard him often enough muttering about getting his own back on enemies in the old country, though he'd built a new life in England.

Ida shifted her weight, the phantom ache from the old ankle injury throbbing in time with her heartbeat, making her reach out to steady herself by gripping the back of a nearby armchair.

'Go on.'

'You know the rest. He's been scheming ever since to build a fortune and bring us down, any way he can. When my father became CEO there were more problems that I've tried to rectify.' Cesare spread his hands in a gesture that opened up those imposing shoulders. 'But Calogero already had his hooks in too deep. There's a liquidity problem. He had the power to destroy the company. Unless I agreed to his terms.'

Ida's hand pressed against her breastbone, holding in her thundering heart. She felt sick. Because, as outlandish as it sounded, she could believe it only too well. Her grandfather was devious and totally ruthless.

'That was the blackmail? Marry me to save the company?'

Cesare narrowed his eyes then shook his head. 'There's no point playing the innocent. He made it clear you're part of this. You know why I married you.'

'To save your family business,' she whispered as the pieces fell into place.

Of course Cesare Brunetti hadn't decided she'd make his ideal wife. That had been foolish naïvety.

What did she have to recommend her? She didn't move in his rarefied circles. She wasn't sophisticated or glamorous. She didn't speak Italian, just a smattering of phrases.

He was powerful and privileged, with the hauteur of a man used to the best of everything.

How had he felt as he'd watched her walk down the aisle on his enemy's arm? The man who threatened the business his family had built and nurtured for generations.

Cesare could probably snap his fingers and have the most gorgeous, talented, interesting women at his beck and call. Why would he want someone who had nothing to recommend her but her eagerness to please?

Ida didn't even have to wonder why her grandfather had lied and said she was a party to the scheme. It was the sort of thing he'd do, to turn the screws and inflame an already dreadful situation. He felt no softness towards her. He didn't even like her.

She doubted Fausto Calogero liked anyone, except maybe Bruno, his head of security. The thought of that brute sent a shudder down her spine.

Cesare returned to the bar, refilling his glass. 'Now that you've stopped pretending—'

'Murder.' Her voice sounded strangled. She swallowed and tried again. 'You said he was a murderer.'

Cesare swung back to her. Something about his expression made her think that for the first time he suspected she didn't know the whole story. It was cold comfort. Nothing could breach the chasm between them now.

'Your grandfather's campaign of revenge wouldn't have worked if he'd just waited, hoping my father would make more bad commercial decisions. He *created* the circumstances that almost ruined us. He had the fire set that burned one of our factories to the ground. Two people died, a security guard who'd been knocked on the head and a manager working late, catching up on paperwork.'

Ida's breath stopped, her fingers clawing the chair's upholstery.

It was one thing to know her grandfather was ruthless and cruel. It was another to hear this.

She had no doubt there was more. Nor did she question Cesare's certainty that her grandfather was behind the arson. It all made a terrible sort of sense as she remembered various cryptic comments she'd overheard.

'Nothing to say? No objections?'

Ida didn't meet his stare. What was the point? She couldn't remember ever feeling so exhausted. So hollow.

Amazing to think that a bare hour ago she'd been excited and optimistic for the future. Her lips twisted in a grimace that matched the wrenching pain deep inside.

'Yet you're doing business with him. You've married his granddaughter.'

He shrugged, those broad shoulders seeming to expand, or maybe it was that her view of the room narrowed. Everything fell away except for this handsome man with a brutally hard expression. Even his perfectly fitted dark suit now looked like a lesson in severity and disdain.

'Doing business with him is necessary if the enterprise my family built over generations is to survive. As for marrying you…' His lips twisted. 'You know that was a condition of the deal. No marriage, no business.'

Cesare paused, his lips turning down as if he too tasted the bitter tang that filled her mouth.

'But you need to know, Ida…' Icy fingers closed around her throat at the sound of her name in that harsh voice. 'I don't take kindly to blackmail. Don't expect me to pander to your whims, or Calogero's.'

Ida met his eyes then, drawn by the sheer depth of hatred in his voice. What she read there stopped any thought of trying, again, to explain that she hadn't been party to her grandfather's schemes. She looked away.

Perhaps, one day, Cesare would hear her out. Not now. Despite the way he leashed his anger, it was clear he was at the edge of his control. She felt his ire in the thickened air like electricity sparking between them.

She sympathised. She'd thought she knew the worst about her grandfather, but these revelations shocked her. She'd learnt to fear the old man. Now she felt ashamed to share his blood.

What else had he done? He'd built a fortune and lived lavishly. Was it all based on criminal activity? No wonder her mother had grabbed the first chance to run away from him. If only Ida had been able to do the same.

She sucked in a breath, trying to calm her rackety pulse. 'What now, Cesare?'

Ida fixed her gaze on the black silk of his bow tie. She couldn't meet his eyes. Not feeling this terrible guilt and horror, the taint of the old man's crimes.

'What now?' Cesare's voice was like that bow tie, smooth and beautiful but severe. 'I don't know what you plan to do but I have calls to make. As for tomorrow...' He paused, and she watched his chest rise on a deep breath as if the prospect of tomorrow was unwelcome. Finally, something they shared! 'Tomorrow we continue the pretence of being a happily married couple.'

'You can't be serious!'

Her gaze shot up, to find him scrutinising her. This time she read nothing in his stare. Not distaste or impatience. Not even anger.

It felt as if he couldn't be bothered wasting his energies on her when he had more important concerns.

'Naturally I'm serious. We agreed to this marriage and now we'll live with it. In public. I have stipulations, of course. Expectations to be met and ground rules you'll need to abide by—'

'Not now,' she whispered, pressing her hand to her churning stomach. 'I'm suddenly very tired.'

Nausea swelled. She'd thought this situation couldn't get worse, but now he asked the impossible. To expect her to act in public as if they had a real marriage while in private they were enemies. To live a pretence of what she'd believed just a short time ago was real...

It was mockery and degradation on top of devastation. Her heart seized up at the very idea.

'Then we'll continue this conversation in the morning.'

Ida swallowed convulsively, forcing back bile at the idea of continuing their discussion. The flesh between her shoulder blades crawled as if an army of spiders danced there.

She turned away, hurrying to her room. But, as in a nightmare, the more urgent her steps the slower she seemed to move.

By the time she finally made it through the open door she almost sobbed her relief. She paused only long enough to snick the lock shut before stumbling to the bathroom.

A scant hour later Ida stood in the centre of the opulent bedroom, checking she hadn't forgotten anything.

Her wedding gown still hung in the wardrobe, as did most of the clothes her grandfather had chosen. There was no point taking more than she could easily carry. She had to travel light, since she'd be hitchhiking.

Stoically she suppressed a jitter of fear at the idea of getting into a car with a stranger. She understood the risks. But the alternative, to stay with a man who despised her, was impossible.

Ida had precious little money. One of her grandfather's methods for keeping her under his thumb had been to ensure she didn't have cash to strike out on her own. Not that it had stopped her trying.

She opened her shoulder bag, checking the contents. Passport. A couple of euro notes, a few pounds, the string of natural pearls her grandfather had produced for her to wear at the wedding. Not because it was an heirloom, precious with family sentiment, but to flaunt his wealth.

Ida's gaze caught on the plain wedding band she wore and the stonking great diamond solitaire beside it. How had she ever imagined Cesare had chosen them as tokens of respect and affection? They were like the pearls. Cold, hard symbols of wealth and ownership.

She'd belonged to a man who'd never cared for her but kept her to use in his obscene scheme. He'd passed her to a man who not only didn't care about her but also actively hated her.

Gritting her teeth, she pulled the rings off and dropped them in her bag, zipping it securely.

She had no idea how much she'd get for the jewellery but selling it was necessary. It would also bring enormous satisfaction.

Ida lifted her other bag off the bed and marched to the door.

CHAPTER THREE

Four years later

CESARE FROWNED AS the limousine turned into a dingy alley. The London downpour was so heavy it should have made everything look cleaner.

Not this place. Even the night failed to soften its squalid edges. Clogged gutters threatened to overflow and, while the road surface glittered slickly, nothing could make these buildings look clean. The neon signs were lurid and the few people on the street reinforced the sleazy atmosphere.

Ida worked *here*?

It didn't make sense. Maybe Calogero *had* told the truth when he said he didn't know where she was. Cesare hadn't believed it.

As the old man's heiress, she had no need to work in this seedy area.

He almost leaned forward to query whether they had the right address, but his staff didn't make such mistakes. Neither his driver nor security staff. Nor the investigators he'd paid handsomely to locate his errant wife.

Wife.

The word sat in the pit of his belly like a lump of cold lead.

In the years since their wedding Ida had never

been a wife. She'd been a resented burden, foisted on him. From the first she'd been a thorn in his side with her almost unconscious sensuality that threatened to seduce him even when he deplored her unscrupulous ways. Only his fury at being forced to marry her had kept him from sleeping with her. Then, with her disappearance four years ago, she'd become a scandal and an embarrassment.

He'd had more important things to do than track her down. Until now.

She was an enemy and an enigma. But only when his investigators reported back had he realised how much of an enigma. Though they'd located her, they hadn't been able to track all her movements through those years. Not surprising when she'd taken a new name not listed on official databases. Yet it was their information about her early life that had astounded him.

Far from growing up in Calogero's London home, after she was orphaned she'd lived most of her life on a remote Scottish island so small it didn't have a regular year-round ferry service. She'd visited London every year, staying with her grandfather for no more than a month each time.

It was bizarre. Almost as bizarre as finding her here.

The car halted. Instantly a woman approached, her red mesh singlet top, vinyl miniskirt and sexualised prowl advertising her profession.

Cesare left it to his bodyguard to send her away

while he got out and strode to the club's narrow entrance. The bouncer, taking in his vehicle and his tailoring, stepped smartly aside.

The dark entry smelled of cigarettes, cheap perfume and alcohol. He strode forward, pushing open a heavy door, and sound hit him. Raucous music and male laughter. Surely the investigators had it wrong. Ida couldn't work here.

His mouth tightened as he took in the pale gleam of gyrating female flesh on what passed for a stage. The other women, some topless, some in what passed, barely, for dresses, were entertaining men at tables around the room.

He'd been warned but he hadn't believed it.

Until his gaze alighted on the bar that ran along one wall and he saw a bright head. A gleam of red-gold, a colour he remembered as clearly as if four years' absence were just four hours. An upright posture, like a dancer's.

The sounds dimmed, replaced by a jackhammering that he eventually registered as his pulse.

It couldn't be her, though the slicked-back hair, pulled tight against her scalp, was the same colour as Ida's. This woman, looking down at the glasses she filled with whisky, wore make-up so bright and heavy she looked like a mannequin. She was all pale skin, scarlet lips and exaggerated eyelashes.

Her black leather lace-up bustier left her shoulders and arms bare and revealed plump breasts on the verge of spilling free.

Even in her translucent-seeming bridal gown Ida hadn't looked so obvious.

Cesare swallowed as he recalled her on their wedding night. She'd dressed for him in blue silk and nothing else. He'd carried that memory ever since.

That night he'd wanted to forget his vow to have nothing to do with the woman who'd been forced on him. He'd wanted to take what she offered. That wanting had fuelled his anger to combustible levels and for the first time since adolescence he'd truly lost his temper.

The woman behind the bar had Ida's colouring but wasn't her. She didn't have that understated allure. She was blatantly, smack-in-the-groin sexy, with her shiny Cupid's bow lips, creamy bosom and narrow waist.

If those weren't blatant enough, she wore long, black gloves past her elbows, that for some reason looked incredibly erotic. As did the black velvet ribbon around her throat.

Was it the contrast of black leather and velvet against soft skin? The thought of his olive-skinned hands touching her pale flesh?

He remembered the contrast when he'd taken Ida's hand in church. Just as he recalled the pillowy softness of her lips beneath his in that perfunctory kiss.

Heat speared his groin, rising to fill his gut in a churn of desperate hunger.

But Cesare didn't do desperate. Especially not

for a tarty barmaid in a dive like this. He was turning when the woman lifted her head and smiled at someone at the end of the bar.

Shock smashed his lungs, stealing his air while his belly clenched in response to the unseen blow.

Ida.

The woman behind the bar, a living, breathing invitation to sex in its raunchiest forms, was his wife!

And he wasn't the only one watching her. Half the men in the place were ogling.

Disbelief vied with distaste and a fury so strong he felt it as a physical surge through his body.

Cesare had been taught to control his impulses, to master anger and think clearly, act logically and honourably. Four years ago, he'd let his control slip and regretted it ever since. Yet as he took in the scene before him it was through a hazy red mist.

It was only when pain shot up his wrists that he realised he'd clenched his hands so tight they throbbed.

Dimly he was aware of a familiar presence beside him. Lorenzo, his chief of security. But this wasn't a matter for staff. This was personal.

Ida was pouring a tray of drinks when she sensed someone approach. Someone who stood close.

Her nape prickled. She'd become better at handling importunate customers with a smile and a quip, and by moving quickly out of reach when necessary, but some of the insistent, aggressive ones scared her.

She glanced to the end of the bar but Mike, the shift manager who sometimes looked out for her, had gone.

She fixed on a careful smile. But it bled from her face as she lifted her eyes, then lifted them further.

White noise rushed in her ears. She had that woozy feeling she recalled from years ago when she'd broken her ankle. She'd looked up from the atrium's marble floor to see her grandfather surveying her coolly from halfway up the staircase and wondered for a second if she'd imagined the slap that had sent her tumbling.

Now she wondered if she could be imagining this.

For the eyes that met hers were familiar. Rich, dark brown eyes that didn't look cold but blazed with heat.

Cesare.

She'd never expected to see him again.

It was her grandfather she was hiding from, not her husband.

Despite her shock, she pulled her lips into a grimace of dark amusement. Cesare had made it abundantly clear he'd be happier without her in his life.

Why was he here?

The whisky bottle thudded onto the bar. There was only one reason he'd come. He must be in London on business and wanted some R and R. Ida had learned in her short time here not to be surprised at the wide range of clientele with a taste for the sordid.

She'd imagined Cesare surrounded by high-society women, the sort who looked like they'd been born wearing haute couture. But maybe he had other predilections.

Her voice was tight as the words jerked out. 'Would you like a drink?'

A bubble of hysterical laughter rose. Where had that come from? Treating him like just another customer.

Was there a chance he wouldn't recognise her? It had been years. The lighting was low, her make-up thick and—

'What I *want* is an explanation. But not here.' He jerked his head towards the door. 'Come on.'

'Sorry?'

Her voice rose and she flinched, sensing heads turning their way.

'We can't talk here.' His lips barely moved, and she realised he spoke through gritted teeth. 'It's time to leave.'

'Maddy?' It was Mike, the shift manager. 'Need help?'

Cesare didn't even look his way. 'She doesn't. This is private family business.'

'Family business? Who are you, her brother?'

Cesare glanced past her then, his look pure macho threat. 'No. Her husband.'

Ida gaped, her mind reeling. The last thing she'd

expected was for Cesare to seek her out, much less claim her as his wife. He was ashamed of her. He hated her!

'Maddy? Is this true?'

She turned to see Mike frowning. He'd taken her under his wing when she'd come to replace Jo. He'd been kind in his own way, and she was grateful.

'Technically, but—'

'It's true,' Cesare said across her, his soft tone threaded with steel. 'And she needs to leave now.'

'Now wait on!' she gasped. He couldn't come here and make demands.

'Alternatively, I have the resources to make business very, very difficult here.' Cesare used the dulcet tone of a man used to getting what he wanted instantly. A man who wouldn't take no for an answer. Those dark eyes moved back to her, fixing her to the spot. 'Is that what you want? For me to bring down a lifetime's trouble on the head of your friend here?'

Ida had never been afraid of Cesare the way she'd been of her grandfather. Both were powerful, single-minded and used to getting their own way, but she'd always felt there was a line Cesare wouldn't cross. She'd never felt physically threatened by him.

Yet looking into those blazing eyes beneath deceptively heavy lids, she saw a man ready to make good on his threat to make trouble. She had no loyalty to the club. She hated the place. But Mike had been good to her and Jo. He didn't deserve trouble.

Plus Jo would return to work here soon and desperately needed the job.

Ida wanted to tell Cesare to go to hell. But if he'd found her here, he'd find her again. Better to discover what he wanted and get it over with. So she shoved down her indignation and shock and turned to Mike.

'It's almost the end of my shift. Could I leave early?'

Ida glanced back at Cesare, noting for the first time the man in the impeccable suit behind him. He was more discreet than her grandfather's bodyguards, but she recognised the type and shivered.

The air was so thick you could cut it with a blade as the men surveyed each other.

Mike broke the silence. 'You're sure, Maddy?'

No, she wasn't. She didn't want to go with Cesare. But the alternative was just as bad. She nodded jerkily.

Why had Cesare come? What did he want?

'Okay. Give me five and I'll get your pay.'

'She doesn't need it,' Cesare said, his voice dripping disdain. 'She—'

'I certainly do need it.' She spoke across him. She hadn't worked here for weeks to walk out with nothing. 'Thanks, Mike.' She smiled at him, her facial muscles stiff. 'I appreciate it.'

With one last, curious look, he headed for the back room.

Ida reached for the whisky to finish pouring drinks. It gave her an excuse not to look at Cesare.

'Leave it! We'll go now.'

His hand shot out to shackle her wrist and she jerked away. '*Don't* touch me, Cesare!'

She half lifted the bottle as if daring him to try and saw surprise widen those narrowed eyes. Behind him his bodyguard shifted as if ready to intervene.

Ida had never hit anyone in her life. The thought made her feel nauseous. But they weren't to know.

How dared he come in here making demands, treating her like a possession? Disrupting her life after all this time?

A bruised corner of her heart silently keened at the way the sight of him opened up all the pain she'd tried to put behind her. She'd told herself that was in the past. That she was over him and that the pain, shame and distress his revelations had caused were long gone.

Now she knew better.

With a shuddering breath that actually hurt, given the tight lacing of Jo's clothes, she broke eye contact, focusing on the whisky.

By some miracle her hand was steady. As if the roiling nerves inside didn't exist. But then, from the age of eight she'd been perfecting the art of not revealing her feelings when she was upset or afraid.

Except with Cesare. That night in Rome he'd undone her with his words and his contempt. Because that day she'd actually imagined herself free from all the bad things, free to start a new life the way she wanted to live it.

'You shouldn't be here.'

His voice was low, rippling over her bare shoulders and the top of her spine like a wintry breeze, drawing her flesh tight.

'It's none of your business.'

She didn't bother looking up, just poured the last glass and slid the tray away, nodding to the waitress who'd come to collect it.

Ida watched the other woman's gaze trace Cesare's tall form, snagging on his wide shoulders in his custom-made suit and that chiselled profile. Finally, after lingering longer than necessary, she lifted the tray and sauntered off with an exaggerated swing of the hips.

'What I do hasn't been your business for four years,' Ida added, turning to put the bottle back.

'That's where you're wrong, Ida. You're still very much my business, whether you want it to be or not.'

She froze, heart hammering against her ribs. Her skimpy outfit was no protection against his scathing stare. She could *feel* it, like an ice cube sliding down her spine and chilling her marrow.

Ida firmed her jaw and lifted her chin. She'd done nothing wrong. She had nothing to be ashamed of.

'Here you are, Maddy.' Mike was at her side, her wages in his big hand. Relief flooded her. For a moment she'd imagined leaving without the cash they needed for the rent. He leaned closer. 'Are you really okay?'

Wordlessly she nodded, his concern touching her.

When she'd first come here Mike, with his brawn and pugnacious air, had made her nervous but she'd been so grateful for his presence.

'Fine, thanks. I'm sorry for leaving early.'

He shook his head. 'Don't fret. But tell Jo to be on time next week.'

She nodded. 'Will do. Bye, Mike. Thanks for everything.'

Cesare's eyes narrowed as he watched the interplay between Ida and the burly guy who'd positioned himself as Ida's champion. Against *him*, her husband!

He felt all sorts of wrong inside. Flummoxed by a riot of unfamiliar feelings. Undone by the surge of anger that, for only the second time he could recall, he had trouble harnessing. The last time had been his wedding night, when Ida had sauntered in, ready for sex, and he'd unleashed his pent-up fury at Calogero's machinations.

He'd been so tempted by her, despite what she represented.

Why was it that with this one woman Cesare's control shattered? At other times his words and actions were careful and considered. He prided himself on his cool head, never being led by emotions.

He'd not have been able to deal with Calogero otherwise.

He watched her shrug into a long raincoat, belting it tight around that narrow waist, and the answer came to him.

Because this woman gets under your skin as no one ever has.

Because you want her. Desperately. Despite who she is and what she's done. Even now, seeing her in this place.

And you hate that need you can't conquer. Because it makes you weak.

Cesare's mood was sombre as they walked through the now sprinkling rain to the limousine. It darkened when she baulked at the open door.

'We'll go back to my hotel,' he murmured, gesturing for her to get in.

'No! Not there.'

Did the idea of being alone with him bother her so much? Her gaze flicked to the car with its door open and driver waiting impassively, then over Cesare's shoulder to where he guessed Lorenzo stood.

'You'll be perfectly safe.'

Safer than here in this insalubrious neighbourhood. The fact she hesitated, as if fearing for her safety with him, felt like a slap in the face.

'There's an all-night café—'

'Absolutely not. I won't have this discussion in public.'

She opened her mouth as if to argue then snapped

it shut. For a moment longer she stared at him from under lowered brows. 'Okay,' she said at last. 'We'll go to mine. It's close.'

Would Joe be there? Cesare had told himself he'd meet Ida briefly and get what he'd come for. Yet now that wasn't enough. His curiosity was aroused. Not least about her man.

'Excellent. I'll look forward to seeing your home.'

Her mouth twisted. She didn't like the idea. Too bad. She wouldn't get rid of him as easily as she'd ditched him four years ago.

He strove to look calm while molten metal poured through his veins. Cesare shouldn't be surprised that she had a lover, yet it felt wrong. He tasted bitterness on his tongue and his hands clenched iron hard.

What sort of man was Joe to let his lover work at a place like that?

Cesare flexed his fingers. He'd soon find out. And on the way he'd try to fathom why it was that, out of all the emotions bombarding him, the strongest felt like jealousy.

He'd never felt possessive of women. He liked their company and enjoyed sex, but he'd never felt strongly enough about one to be jealous. For that he could thank his father, whose disastrous mistakes of judgement served as a horrible warning.

Cesare's nape prickled at the idea he was envious of the man who shared Ida's bed. Until he realised it wasn't personal. It was simply because, though he didn't like her, Ida was still his wife.

His.

Wife.

All those traditional mores around fidelity sprang to the fore, as if within the modern man dwelt the sort of traditional male who'd lived generations before.

But then, as his mother had died when he was a baby and his father had abandoned him to follow a series of ever more unsuitable women, he'd been raised by his grandfather. The old man had instilled a sense of family honour in Cesare, hence his determination to save the family business no matter what the cost.

Could those values really be why he hadn't taken a lover since their farce of a wedding? No, that was just because he'd had other priorities these past four years.

'Are you ready?' he murmured when still she didn't move.

'What is it you want?' she whispered.

Cesare's patience wore thin. After the way she'd run in the night and the huge scandal he'd had to weather, she begrudged him one face-to-face chat?

'We'll discuss it in private. Not on the street.'

With one last, frowning glance, she got in.

The flash of long, slender legs in fishnet tights beneath her drab raincoat was a punch to the belly. Or perhaps to his pride.

He didn't want Ida in his life. Never had. Yet the idea his wife, the woman on whom he'd bestowed the proud Brunetti name, was shacked up with an-other man and working as a prostitute, or something close, shattered his dignity.

Cesare slid into the seat after her, stretching his legs as she gave her address to his driver.

It was good they wouldn't see each other again after tonight. He didn't like the heated, uncomfort-able emotions she stirred.

So it was a surprise when, as they drove through the dark, wet streets of London, he found himself thinking, not of the business he'd come to finalise, but about the one thing pride and common sense dictated was off-limits. How satisfying it would be to strip Ida slowly bare.

He'd remove one item of provocative clothing at a time before losing himself in the soft, slick warmth of her femininity. He'd listen to her gasps as he pleasured her and hear the sound of his name, only his, on her lips, as he took her to screaming climax again and again before finding his own completion.

Cesare's breath atrophied in his lungs and he had to drag in oxygen, his heart hammering, his groin tight as if gripped by a vice.

It was good that his self-control was strong enough to withstand such tawdry temptation.

Wasn't it?

CHAPTER FOUR

HER NEIGHBOURHOOD WAS worse than he'd expected. It wasn't a street where anyone would choose to live.

Cesare recognised the signs from some of the community building work he'd done, part of his grandfather's determination to ensure he didn't grow up as an entitled kid with no idea how the other half lived. It had been hands-on work and had left him with a respect for those who survived the difficult circumstances life threw at them. And a distaste for those who preyed on the vulnerable. The pimps, pushers and stand-over men.

Was Joe Ida's pimp? Ice crackled along his bones at the idea.

She'd been selling drinks, not her body at the club, but in a place like that lines blurred. She dressed as if she were for sale.

His belly cramped down on nausea as he followed her into a cement shell of a foyer then up a couple of flights of bare steps. His nose wrinkled at the smell of the stained walls.

Easier to think about the rundown building than Ida's slim, net-clad legs in those ridiculously high patent leather shoes. Or the possibility that she sold more than drinks at that club.

She stopped outside a dingy door and fumbled

with the key. Did she have cold fingers because of her skimpy clothes? Or was she nervous?

The possibility took Cesare aback.

Earlier Ida had been wary but not afraid. He'd read surprise when she saw him, swiftly followed by indignation and resentment. She was clearly a woman used to standing up for herself. Nothing like the fake innocent she'd played before their wedding.

She pushed the door open but it jammed, a chain rattling across the gap.

'Jo? It's me.'

At the sound of the guy's name a confusing welter of feelings rose. So Joe was in the flat.

Cesare moved closer then wished he hadn't when he caught the fresh scent of hyacinths. As if Ida had been working in a spring garden instead of a strip club.

There was another rattle then the door opened so Ida could slip in. It was already closing when Cesare jammed his foot in the gap.

'It's okay, Jo, he's with me.'

Cesare's half-formed assumptions about her boyfriend died as he shouldered his way in and saw the figure behind the door. A slender woman with a short cap of black hair, wary eyes and a massive bruise fading to yellow all down one side of her face. She looked about sixteen. Until he looked closer and realised she was much older.

Her face was taut with surprise melded with anxiety as her gaze climbed to meet his eyes.

'I mean no harm,' he murmured, instinctively seeking to reassure.

She said nothing but jerked her head once and turned to shut the door. The chain and a bolt had been inexpertly fitted and, by the look of it, recently. Instinct prickled. What had prompted its installation?

'I'm Cesare Brunetti.'

Slowly he held out his hand. The girl looked at it for what seemed an age then slipped her hand in his. 'Jo Randall.'

Jo? Not Joe, as he'd assumed?

Rapidly Cesare recalculated. He'd jumped to conclusions. How many of his assumptions were wrong? The possibility disturbed him.

He strode after Ida, determined to get answers, and almost bumped into her. The flat was tiny and a couple of paces took him halfway across the room.

He surveyed it in a glance. Cramped but with a surprisingly welcoming air, due, he realised, to the clever use of paint and soft furnishings in terracotta and pale citrus that drew attention from the old, mismatched furniture.

But his attention was on Ida, putting her bag on a small table and opening her raincoat. He caught a glimpse of creamy flesh and fishnet stockings and hurriedly lifted his gaze to her face. Her make-up looked even more garish under the overhead light.

She wasn't looking at him. 'What are you doing

here, Jo? Did something go wrong at work?' Ida's voice was low as she drew the young woman aside.

Cesare wasn't into eavesdropping. But the space was too small for privacy, though the women spoke in whispers. There was some problem with work, and money.

He took a few steps away, as if inspecting the combined kitchen, living and dining room, taking in the curtain across one end of the room. To partition off a sleeping space?

He frowned. This wasn't how he'd expected Ida to live. She was Calogero's heiress. This only deepened the mystery of her work in a sleazy bar.

Cesare swung around. As if sensing his movement, both women turned to look at him.

He'd waited long enough. They had business to settle, and he chafed to get it over with. But Cesare refused to conduct his business with a stranger listening.

'Ida, we need to talk. Alone.'

Ida glowered as if wishing him anywhere but here, but finally she nodded. He saw her pass the envelope with her wages to Jo.

'Okay. Let's go.'

'Wait.' Jo put a hand on Ida's arm, her gesture and tone urgent. 'Why did he call you Ida?'

Cesare watched emotions flicker across his wife's face, too fast to read.

Finally she shrugged and spread her hands. 'It doesn't matter, Jo.' She paused then went on, as if recognising that her friend deserved more, 'It's my first name. But I haven't used it in ages because I wanted a fresh start. My middle name is Madeline, so I've been Maddy for four years.'

Yet the question was why she'd thought it necessary to hide her identity in London. Who or what was she afraid of?

Him? The idea made Cesare's skin crawl.

But it was hard to believe. He'd been blisteringly furious that night in Rome but, though he'd shocked her with his refusal to sleep with her, he hadn't aimed to frighten her. Nor could she have expected him to seek her out. He'd made it clear he wasn't interested.

Besides, he'd been busy for four years fighting tooth and nail to claw back control of the family's luxury goods company from under Calogero's nose. That had left precious little time for wondering about his missing spouse. The old man had been furious at her disappearance but the legal contract he and Cesare had signed meant he hadn't been able to liquidate the company as he'd threatened. No doubt that infuriated him even more. He'd given up some of his leverage for social gain that hadn't materialised.

'Your name's really Ida?' Her flatmate didn't seem upset at the deceit.

'It doesn't make any difference, Jo.'

'But it *does*. There was a man looking for you.'

'A man?' Ida and Cesare spoke together.

'What man?' Ida took a step nearer her friend, her voice sharp. 'Did he come to the door?'

'No, he was at the entrance to the building, asking if anyone knew an Ida.'

Cesare watched Ida's complexion turn chalky white beneath her make-up and took a step nearer. 'When was this?'

'Yesterday.' Jo looked from Ida to him then back. 'I would have mentioned it if I'd known.'

'You weren't to know.' Ida shook her head. 'But he definitely asked for me by name? You're *sure* it was Ida?'

Jo nodded. 'I'm sure. He waved a photo under my nose, but I didn't really look because he scared me and I wanted to get away. But I did glimpse rose-gold hair like yours.'

She stopped at Ida's quick intake of breath.

'Was he working for you?' Ida spun around. Those light green eyes snared his with an intensity he felt to the soles of his feet. 'Cesare?'

He shook his head. 'No. My investigators located you a while ago, but they had instructions not to approach.'

Because this was business he preferred to conduct in person. He'd only arrived in Britain today, ostensibly for commercial reasons, but the most compelling was to settle things with Ida.

'So if he doesn't work for you...'

He saw her swallow and reach for the back of a chair, fingers gripping so tight they looked bloodless.

'What did he look like, Jo, do you remember?'

'Not nice,' came the immediate answer. 'That's why I remember so well. Short-cropped hair and a nose that had been broken a couple of times. He wore a suit, but he was so bulky his arms were like hams, and he looked like he had no neck.' She paused, her breath hitching. 'He had a voice like the bottom of a gravel pit, and I didn't like the way he looked at me.'

Ida sank onto the spindly chair. The movement was so abrupt Cesare guessed her knees had folded involuntarily.

He moved forward but made room for Jo to crouch before her. 'Maddy? Ida…are you okay?'

Clearly the answer was no. He saw a shudder rack her whole frame. Yet to his surprise Ida nodded, her mouth drawing up in a weak approximation of a smile.

'Of course. I just got a surprise.'

'It's someone you know,' Cesare interjected.

She kept her eyes on her flatmate. 'Just someone from the past I'd rather not run into.'

Which meant, since she hadn't used her real name in four years, that it was someone from before their wedding. An ex-boyfriend? Surely not with that description.

'Time enough to worry about him tomorrow,' she added, her false cheer so jarring that Cesare's hackles rose.

'I haven't seen the guy since,' Jo offered. 'Maybe he's left the area.'

Cesare crossed his arms, taking in the contradiction of Ida's hunched shoulders and fake smile. It was obvious she didn't want anyone prying and discovering her secrets.

It seemed his dear wife had more than one skeleton in her closet.

Technically he didn't need to uncover those secrets. He could finalise what he'd come to do quickly and be gone.

Yet from the first, Ida with her machinations and mysteries had got under his skin like a burr under a saddle. If he intended to eradicate her from his life, he needed to lay those truths completely bare so he could move on.

Maybe this wasn't going to be sorted as quickly as he'd planned.

Ida shifted on the limousine's soft leather seat, her limbs stiff with stress and the effort of fighting a chill that seemed to come from her bones. She wrapped her arms around her torso and folded her legs together.

Too late she'd realised her mistake in leaving the flat in the clothes she'd worn to the club. But she'd been too dazed to think of changing.

She should have demanded they talk in her flat as planned. She didn't like the idea of going to *his* suite, being on *his* territory.

But she'd shied away from reliving her embarrassing history with him before anyone, even a friend like Jo. Ida felt scraped raw whenever she thought of their catastrophic wedding day, her naïvety and Cesare's expression as he'd shredded her tentative hopes. His scorn had been like acid on soft flesh and her even softer heart.

On top of that, the news that her grandfather's henchman was searching for her had scrambled her brain. Jo's description fitted Bruno perfectly. It was hard to think when fear gripped her lungs like a vice.

She swallowed, her throat scratchy as if lined with emery. Bruno.

The man who for years had either looked right through her or, occasionally, directly at her like a starving bulldog slavering over a piece of meat.

No wonder she'd let Cesare lead her to his car without protest. She could only be grateful he'd left his bodyguard to keep an eye on the flat lest Bruno return. Cesare's thoughtfulness in protecting Jo had been unexpected. The flat that had been her refuge now felt flimsy and unsafe. Bruno was looking for her, right at her building, and she was terrified.

Ida shuddered as memories teased her. The way her grandfather had squashed her tentative bid for a little freedom when she was sixteen. He'd threatened to teach her obedience by giving her to Bruno, his hulk of a bodyguard, for a night.

She'd seen Bruno in action with anyone who got

too close to Fausto Calogero. The ex-convict was quick and violent. That afternoon he'd leered and licked his lips ostentatiously as he'd stripped her naked with his eyes. Then the two men had laughed as she'd scurried to her room.

You think you're safer with Cesare Brunetti?

The voice in her head goaded and she turned, surveying the figure on the other side of the seat. Even in the gloom he looked imposing as he ignored her, talking on the phone in low, liquid Italian. Her heart gave a little fluttery roll as passing lights defined his handsome, hard profile.

Some things hadn't changed.

She hated the way she still felt vulnerable around him, those old hormonal responses still there under the surface. But surely that was just a sense memory, a remnant of the crush she'd once had on him.

More importantly she *did* feel safe with him.

He might be cold and condescending. They might detest each other. But Cesare Brunetti wasn't like her grandfather or Bruno. He wasn't violent. He wasn't a criminal with no compunction.

What was the worst he could do to her? Give her a stern talking-to?

Ida thought of the way he'd spoken to Jo, reassuring her, taking his time to put her at ease. He'd made it seem easy, which was remarkable given his impressive height and Jo's nervousness after the assault that had left her battered and wary.

Ida closed her eyes and let her head loll against the back of the seat.

She'd told herself for so long that she was free of Cesare. He'd probably instituted divorce proceedings the day she left. He'd certainly washed his hands of her, and she was glad.

Yet from the moment tonight when she'd looked up into dark velvet eyes, she'd realised that was a lie.

In four years she hadn't dated. She'd told herself she was too busy keeping a roof over her head and food in her body, but that unmistakable sensation of heat unfurling as she met Cesare's eyes gave another reason.

However much she disliked the man, she was still attracted to him.

What a nightmare!

Could tonight get any worse?

'We're here.'

That deep voice lassoed her around the middle, pulling tight as if to draw her close. Ida snapped her eyes open and goggled when she saw where they were.

A man in a long uniform coat and tall hat opened the door. 'Ma'am.'

He didn't precisely bow, but his gesture was a mixture of welcome and deference, and she found herself swinging her legs out of the car, grateful she still wore her raincoat over the fishnet tights and ultra-short miniskirt.

'Thank you.'

Then Cesare was beside her. He looped her arm through his and they stepped into a world of hushed luxury.

Ida had never been here, but she'd heard of this iconic hotel. She could only be thankful that at this hour the foyer was empty.

A receptionist greeted them, but Ida kept her head averted, conscious of the image she projected with her laden make-up and hated fishnets.

Ida had never liked the limelight. She wasn't shy but for most of her life she'd felt like she didn't belong.

Her mouth twisted. Here it was the truth. She did *not* belong in one of the country's most exclusive hotels.

Yet Ida refused to let Cesare know how weary and nervous she felt. She stiffened her backbone.

She'd get through the next half-hour, deal with whatever problem Cesare posed and then go home, ditch the make-up and awful clothes, and work out what to do about Bruno.

Ida barely noticed the beautiful furnishings as they reached Cesare's suite and he shut the door behind them. But she did take in the size of the sitting room—it was big enough to fit her flat six times over—and the faint scent of lilies and luxury. For a weak moment she contemplated dropping onto one of the cream lounges and shutting eyes scratchy with exhaustion. It had been a long time since she'd started her dawn cleaning shift.

Instead, she strolled into the room then twisted around to face her companion, ignoring the burn where the borrowed shoes rubbed her heels.

'Okay. We're alone. Why did you come looking for me?'

'I thought that was obvious.'

How could she have forgotten the intensity of that brooding stare? Cesare's eyes bored into hers as if seeking out misdemeanours or weaknesses.

But she'd done him no wrong. She didn't owe him anything and refused to be cowed by that flinty gaze. She shoved her hands deep in her raincoat pockets and raised her eyebrows.

'It's been a long day, Cesare. I'm not in the mood for guessing games. Just tell me. What do you want?'

He crossed the space between them in a couple of deceptively easy strides. Deceptive because his expression told her it was the prowl of a predator.

'To sort out our divorce, of course.'

CHAPTER FIVE

'WE'RE STILL MARRIED?'

Her hand went to her throat and Cesare was torn between the idea she was shocked and knowing she had to be faking.

'Of course we're married. You haven't signed divorce papers, have you?'

She shook her head, her glossy lips opening then closing. Those exaggerated eyelashes fluttered, and he almost thought he saw the movement echoed in the pulse point at her throat, so convincing was her show of surprise.

She was a fine actress. Though in retrospect she'd slightly overdone the role of shy innocent when they'd met.

What role was she playing now? Not the ingenue, given what he'd seen tonight.

Abruptly she sank onto the sofa behind her. It wasn't a graceful movement and made him think she really had been taken by surprise. As when she'd heard someone was searching for her.

Once again, he experienced a sharp pang that felt like concern.

It annoyed him. His concern was for his extended family, his employees and investors. It shouldn't be for this woman who'd been foisted on him, an insult to add to the injury Calogero had done his family.

Cesare turned on his heel and crossed to the bar. He took his time pouring two glasses of Sambuca before returning to where she sat, head bent, arms wrapped around her middle.

'Here.' He pushed the glass into her hand. 'This will warm you.'

Despite his impatience she worried him. This was the second time he'd seen her turn parchment pale, making her heavy make-up appear even more false against the delicate curves of her cheeks and lips.

Cesare took the seat opposite, eyes narrowing as she lifted her face.

'I assumed you'd divorced me four years ago.'

'When you left me high and dry for all the world to gossip about? The bridegroom with no bride.'

That still stung. One more debt to lay at her door. He was a proud man. Having acquaintances and even people he didn't know sniggering up their sleeves at him had been hard to endure.

'You didn't want a bride! You made that clear.'

'There's a difference between not wanting you and having you disappear off the face of the earth. Don't you have any regrets over the scandal you caused? The speculation and rumours? You dropped me into a hell of a mess.'

As if he hadn't been busy enough saving the family company and all those jobs, independent of Calogero. He'd had the fallout of a missing bride with the world agog for stories of Cesare Brunetti and his new wife. His plan had been to maintain the fiction of a happy marriage though in fact it would be in name only. Then he'd divorce her as soon as he could erase Calogero's influence from his life.

Ida sipped her drink then grimaced and shuddered as if she'd never drunk alcohol.

'You should have thought of that before you treated me as a whipping boy for my grandfather.'

He should indeed. He'd made the mistake of letting the anger he'd tamped down for so long finally get the better of him. It was a brief loss of control that he'd lived to regret.

But what intrigued him was that Ida said it to his face. She'd changed from the woman he'd known.

Of course she has. She's stopped pretending butter wouldn't melt in her mouth.

'You knew there was no divorce. There's been no paperwork.'

Ida took another sip. 'I don't know the process.' She lifted one shoulder. 'What? I've never been divorced before.'

'And you're not yet. That's why I'm here.'

'It took you long enough.'

She sounded belligerent, as if *he'd* let *her* down. The gall of the woman!

'I had a few things to keep me busy.' Like turning around the enterprise Calogero had sabotaged and finding ways to create the profits it needed without his nemesis realising Cesare's plan to oust him. 'What's your excuse?'

Her eyes met his in a flash of fire that reminded

him of green-tinged clouds that presaged summer thunderstorms in his beloved Tuscany. That green tint was a warning of a dangerous electrical storm to follow.

'It never occurred to me that you'd let the marriage stand. I was sure you'd arrange a divorce or an annulment. The marriage wasn't consummated.'

Cesare's nostrils flared on a sharp inward breath.

He could imagine the gossip if he'd tried to end their union that way. There'd be salacious speculation about why they hadn't slept together. No one would believe it was because he wouldn't touch his pretty little bride. Not when every man at the wedding, and untold others who'd seen the media photos, had been busy imagining themselves in Cesare's position, stripping that diaphanous bridal gown off her slender body.

He lifted his glass and tossed back the fiery aniseed alcohol.

The burn down his throat was the distraction he needed from the well-worn direction of his thoughts. It was too easy imagining himself helping Ida out of her wedding dress or that slinky nightdress that had provoked him, finally, into losing his cool.

Cesare looked at his empty glass, surprised that he'd finished it. Moderation in all things was his motto, learned from his beloved grandfather and reinforced by his father's appalling example.

Cesare always stood strong in the face of provocation and temptation. Even when, in Ida's case, he'd teetered on the brink.

'That's why I'm here. To sort out the divorce.'

The sooner the better. After four years' absence this woman still messed with his head. It was inexplicable.

'Good.' She put down her drink and sat forward. 'Where do I sign?'

Cesare had expected prevarication or pleas. Coaxing or apologies. Not eagerness.

He struggled not to betray his stupefaction. 'You agree to the divorce?'

'Of course.'

For the first time tonight those amazing eyes looked clear and unguarded. Her plush mouth even crooked at the corners. As if it was the best news she could imagine.

Cesare leaned back, surprised.

She was giving him what he wanted. What he *needed*. Yet he hadn't been prepared for it to be so easy. He'd expected her consent to cost him.

Had he *wanted* her to object? Was her enthusiasm a blow to his pride?

He was accustomed to women trying to persuade him to extend their time together, though admittedly that hadn't been for a while. The last four years he'd had no time for women, devoting his energy to wresting the company free of Calogero's clutches.

Maybe his appeal had diminished in that time?

Though, recalling the way Ida had eaten him up with her eyes earlier, he couldn't believe it.

Four years of abstinence did, however, explain his response to her. He was a healthy man with a healthy interest in a sexy woman. He didn't like or approve of Ida, but he couldn't deny she was sexy. He refused to countenance the idea that he'd been celibate so long because he'd been fixated on her.

She'd opened that shabby raincoat in the warmth of the suite and as she leaned forward he had a view of white breasts that was impossible to ignore. That bustier was cut so low and pushed her bounty so high that it looked like her nipples would burst free of their confinement at any moment.

He had to forcibly drag his gaze up, only to find it snagging on glossy, full red lips that made him think of searing, straight-to-the-groin orgasm.

Heat flared, his body tightening and his throat turning arid.

In one swift movement he rose and made for the bar.

'Another?' he asked over his shoulder, his voice grating.

'No, thanks. One's my limit.'

Cesare bit back the urge to tell her it was too late to play at inexperience. Not when he'd found her pouring shots in a strip club. But why waste energy?

He took his time pouring the drink. When he turned around the raincoat was open a little more, treating him to a view of long legs clad in fishnet stockings.

If asked, he would have said his taste ran to women whose sensuality was more discreet and refined. Tonight, he realised he was as responsive as the next man to pale flesh in black leather and provocative high heels.

His fingers tightened around the glass, but he refused to swallow the drink in one. He didn't need alcohol as a prop. He could easily withstand Ida's obvious attractions.

'I have the papers.'

He pulled them out and dropped them onto the coffee table before her, then took the seat opposite. Only then did he allow himself a tiny sip of his drink. Its warm bite dragged his attention from his heavy groin.

Ida picked up the papers and scanned them, turning page after page. She really was keen to sign, flipping quickly to the end. Cesare reached in his pocket for a pen but paused as she spoke.

'I can't sign these.'

Ah, as he expected. She wouldn't make this easy. Now came the play for a better financial settlement, despite the watertight prenup they'd signed.

Something like relief settled inside him at the realisation he'd had her pegged right.

'I'm sure you can.' With the right incentive. Like knowing he wasn't going to renegotiate. He placed his pen on the low table before her. 'You wanted a divorce. Here's your chance.'

She dropped the papers on the table, her mouth twisting. 'Much as I'd love to oblige you, it's not possible. These are in Italian.'

Cesare watched her sit back, folding her arms and pushing her breasts higher.

He swallowed. Such obvious tactics wouldn't work. 'And that's a problem because?'

'I don't understand Italian.'

Cesare stared. It was true that before the wedding they'd always spoken English. 'But the wedding service was all in Italian.'

She shrugged. 'I practised. My grandfather wanted me word perfect.'

But it wasn't just the church service. 'You had no trouble signing the prenuptial contract. You didn't ask for an English version.'

He and her grandfather had watched her sign the agreement. She'd simply picked up the pen, glanced at the document and signed in her neat, round hand.

'That was different.'

Cesare raised his eyebrows. 'I don't see how.'

Those pale green eyes met his, her look haughty. 'My grandfather and his lawyer had already been through the contract.'

Cesare would never sign anything without reading and understanding it himself. 'You left it to them? They explained it all to you?'

That didn't fit with his memory. There'd been

changes made just before the meeting. He'd watched old Calogero read that section carefully before passing it to her to sign. 'Or are you saying you signed it without understanding it?'

Surely that wasn't normal for a gold-digger?

Abruptly she shifted, pulling her coat closer.

'What do you care, Cesare? I signed your all-important prenup, so you're safe. I'm not going to take you to the cleaners with this divorce.' She huffed out a breath. 'But I'm not signing this until it's translated. I could be signing *anything*!' He opened his mouth, but before he could speak she went on. 'I want an English copy, not for someone to read the Italian and explain what it means.'

She thought he was trying to dupe her? That he'd lie about the contents?

His hackles rose. The Brunettis did not do business that way. He was neither a bully nor a criminal like her grandfather.

Which means you respect her right to sign a document she can understand.

'So be it.'

He finished his drink and slammed the glass down, glancing at his watch. It was well into the early hours of the morning.

'It will take some time to get a translation.'

Ida nodded, rising in one supple movement. 'Call me when—'

'No, Ida.' Cesare was beside her in a moment. 'You'll wait here until the translation's made.'

'I beg your pardon?'

Her freezing tone would have done an empress proud.

'You don't think I'm letting you out of my sight before you sign on the dotted line? Not with your record of vanishing without warning.'

Ida's head tipped back as she met his eyes. Even in these teetering heels she didn't come near his height. He was taller, physically stronger and had a brooding air of ruthlessness that made her blood slow in her veins to a heavy, warning beat.

'You really mean it!'

He inclined his head. 'I never say things I don't mean.'

'You know where I live. I'm not going anywhere.'

He shook his head. 'I learned my mistake with you in Rome. I won't make the same mistake twice.'

Ida rubbed her arms through the thin coat. 'That makes no sense. I want a divorce too. I won't disappear.'

'So you say.' His words fell like lead weights in the thickened atmosphere. 'But I'm taking no chances.'

He didn't believe her.

Ida smoothed her coat down, at the same time drawing herself taller. 'You're not the only one who isn't in the habit of saying what they don't mean. I don't lie.' She paused but saw no softening in that sharp stare. 'Anyway, I have to work.'

'You've just finished work.'

She rolled her eyes. 'I have two jobs.' More than two, actually. And though Jo had taken on some of her night cleaning shifts while she'd filled in for Jo at the bar, Ida still worked through the day.

'Tell them you'll be in the next day instead.'

As if! Her work was cash in hand. No sick days or time off. She worked hard and did a good job, but if her clients thought her unreliable they'd get someone else.

'This isn't worth arguing about.' Ida belted her raincoat. 'I can be back here around three in the afternoon. Will that give you time to get the translation?'

'I'm sure it will.' He moved between her and the door. 'But you'll stay here until then.' He cut off her protest. 'There's a spare bedroom and bathroom.'

His phone rang just as she was about to tell him what she thought of that idea. He pulled it from his pocket, frowned at the caller ID and lifted it to his ear.

Indignation rose. He didn't even have the decency to ignore his phone while he made his outrageous demands.

Ida stalked past him, only to slam to a halt as a hand wrapped around her wrist.

Shock filled her.

At that unexpected, unwanted touch.

And at the heat rippling under her skin. A sensation that had less to do with outrage and more to do with awareness.

Something needy stirred. Something she'd told herself she'd imagined from her short time with Cesare. It was wholly feminine, responding even to his harsh, take-charge masculinity. She hated this weakness.

She swung around, lifting her hand, about to break his hold, when she read his expression.

He spoke in Italian, brusque and decisive, then ended the call. 'You know this man?'

He held out the phone and Ida's blood froze at the image there.

Bruno. Her grandfather's enforcer.

Bruno on the street outside her flat, and a second photo of him outside this magnificent hotel.

Her breath stopped.

He knew where she was. Which meant her grandfather did too. She wasn't safe.

Ida swayed and this time Cesare's hold wasn't imprisoning but supportive. Dimly she was aware of him tossing his phone aside and grabbing her elbows as stress took its inevitable toll and her knees gave way.

The world rolled and she found herself floating off the floor, pressed tight against Cesare's hard chest, his powerful arms embracing her.

She caught a hint of that lemon, cedar and man scent she remembered from years ago, and squeezed her eyes shut against an overwhelming barrage of sensations.

When she opened them he was sitting on a sofa and she was across his lap, tucked into his embrace, the thrum of his heart steady beneath her ear.

She felt undone. Tonight had been one shock after another. Her hard-won defences were unravelling, and her strength with them.

She should be pushing free, getting off Cesare's lap and leaving.

But where would she go?

Was Bruno out there, waiting for her?

A shudder racked her and Cesare's arms tightened. Ida told herself she didn't like or trust this man, but it was impossible to regret the comfort of his firm hold.

It felt bizarrely as if he could keep her safe.

He who'd hurt her so badly!

'It's the same man, isn't it?'

She nodded. 'Who took the photos? The man you left behind at the flat?'

'Lorenzo is head of my security team. He saw this guy watch us leave your flat and follow us here. Lorenzo tailed him.'

Cesare paused as if expecting her to explain. But her mind was racing, grappling with the implications.

She'd have to move. Start again.

She couldn't afford to let Bruno catch her. The

air thickened, pressing down on her as black spots danced before her eyes.

Her grandfather would be furious at the way she'd deserted her marriage when he'd aimed to build on that to stake a place for himself in the society that had rejected him for so long. His rage would be monumental, and his vengeance didn't bear thinking about.

If she continued to flat-share with Jo she would put her friend at risk too.

Ida put her fingertips to her forehead, her pulse beating so hard at her temples she felt sick.

For four years she'd managed, just, to keep her head above water. She'd stayed safe, found a home and work. She'd even added to her slim savings in the hopes of eventually moving to the countryside, once she had enough money to start again.

Now her hopes were shattered. With Bruno on her trail, she had to leave immediately and start somewhere new. Where would she go? Where would she be safe?

'Talk to me, Ida.'

It should feel odd, sharing information with this man, but for some reason it didn't. 'He works for my grandfather.'

'I remember his face. Your grandfather's body-guard.'

'That's part of his role.'

Thug. Stand-over man. Enforcer. Gaoler. Bruno was adaptable.

She shivered and Cesare again tightened his hold. Strange that now his touch didn't feel like imprisonment but protection.

But then, there was nothing like the fear of imminent violence to clarify your priorities. She didn't like Cesare Brunetti but she didn't fear him.

Cesare felt the shivers course through her slender body.

'You're scared.'

Which made the tight tug of material at his crotch an embarrassment. He shouldn't lust after a woman who was shivering with fear, no matter how good she felt against his body.

'He's not a nice man.'

The way she said it made his nape tingle. Beneath her calm tone was an unmistakeable thread of terror.

'Is it him you're scared of or your grandfather?'

Her head tipped back so that her face turned up to his. He saw shimmering ruby lips. Thick make-up and exaggerated lashes that earlier had made her eyes look slumbrous and heavy. Now as he met those pale mint-green eyes he read not defiance or indignation but distress.

His pulse stuttered in shock.

Because his overwhelming impulse was to shelter her.

Closely followed by the urge to settle his mouth over those plush lips and delve deep, to see if she tasted as honey-sweet as he remembered from their kiss in the church.

Had the appalling London weather shorted his brain?

'Does it matter?'

Technically, no. Except something had changed tonight. From the moment Cesare had discovered Ida in that dingy club everything had become complicated. His response to her wasn't what he'd anticipated.

Now he'd discovered another mystery.

There was something between Ida and her grandfather that he needed to understand because bringing down Fausto Calogero was his top priority. Anything concerning the old devil was vital information.

Then there was the mystery of Ida herself. What was she hiding? Why, after what she'd done, did he respond so viscerally to her?

He couldn't in good conscience walk away and leave her terrified. Which all added up to one solution. Outlandish but unavoidable.

'Forget staying here overnight. Or,' he added when she moved as if to stand up, 'coming back at three. Do you have a current passport?'

Those clear eyes widened. But instead of questioning him Ida slowly nodded.

Half an hour ago she'd have protested that she wouldn't go anywhere with him.

'I'll have Lorenzo go to your flat and get it.'

She breathed deep, her soft breast pushing against his chest and messing with his head. But for once he was sure that wasn't intentional. Nor was the nervous way she moistened her lips with the tip of her tongue. Ida was truly terrified.

'There's no need. I always carry my passport with me.'

That, more than anything else he'd seen tonight, proved her desperation. Unless she travelled constantly, which, given her circumstances, wasn't an option, there was only one reason for that. Because she was always prepared for a quick getaway.

That solidified his sudden decision.

'Good. You're coming with me to Italy. Now.'

CHAPTER SIX

IDA WOKE TO the sound of someone moving about in her room.

Heart pounding, she jack-knifed up, wisps of nightmare still fogging her brain.

The fine cotton sheet slid against her skin and she realised she was naked. Instantly she clawed the sheet up around her shoulders.

Her breath sighed out as she realised she wasn't in her cramped flat with its flimsy front door. The noise wasn't her grandfather's henchman breaking in.

Gradually her racing pulse eased.

Instead of seeing a tiny sliver of louring London sky, bright sunshine flooded across the honey-coloured wooden floor and a sumptuous antique carpet of blush roses on a cream background. A trim, grey-haired woman drew the floor-length curtains open.

Ida shaded her eyes. Through the tall windows was a cerulean sky with a single puffy cloud, cotton wool against the vibrant blue.

'I'm sorry to wake you, *signora*. I've brought you a late breakfast.' She nodded to a laden tray on a nearby table. 'Signor Brunetti asked me to wake you so you can freshen up before the lawyer arrives at midday.'

Midday? Ida was usually working at dawn. She *never* slept in.

But last night, or rather this morning, had been remarkable, she realised as impressions crowded her brain.

Cesare's astounding determination to spirit her out of London. The ease with which he'd organised transport in the dead of night. A limousine to the airport, a private flight to Florence then a helicopter to his country home.

Most remarkable of all was the fact that she'd acquiesced! As if she were used to letting someone else take charge. As if every day wasn't about the struggle to be free to make her own decisions.

As if she trusted Cesare Brunetti.

What choice had she had? Faced with either her unwanted husband or Bruno, there'd been no choice.

Besides, there was something powerfully appealing about, just once, having someone else solve her problems, albeit temporarily.

A shiver skated down her spine. It was a weakness she couldn't afford to foster.

Deliberately she shut her mind against thoughts of the other weakness she felt around Cesare Brunetti. The insidious desire that still haunted her.

'Thank you. I shouldn't have slept so long.' She paused, uncomfortable. She wasn't used to servants. The only person who occasionally saw her in bed was Jo if their shifts worked out that way. 'I don't know your name.'

'I'm Dorotea, the housekeeper.' The woman smiled, though her eyes were wary. 'Welcome to Tuscany, Signora Brunetti.'

Signora Brunetti!

Ida snapped her gaping mouth shut.

Why would Cesare reveal her identity? He wanted to end their marriage as soon as possible.

'Thank you, Dorotea. Have we met before?' Ida had never visited this house.

'No, but I recognise you from your wedding photos in the press. Such a beautiful bride! It's a pleasure to welcome you here at last.'

'Thank you very much.'

Ida blushed, realising what had seemed simple and expedient last night brought with it a stack of complications.

She hadn't just escaped Bruno. She'd walked into the role of Cesare's wife.

Had he intended that? What was the real reason he'd helped her?

She recalled his scathing expression the night he'd revealed his true feelings for her. That meant his actions last night had been on the spur of the moment too.

Yet he seemed the sort of man who didn't leave anything to chance.

She pushed her hair off her face, fingers tangling in waves still tacky from the product she'd used to slick down her hair yesterday. After clients at the bar had grabbed at her hair to haul her close, she'd opted for a severe hairstyle there.

Now she regretted she hadn't washed her hair last night. She'd been so weary she'd cleaned off her make-up, stripped off her borrowed clothes and fallen naked into bed.

'Signor Brunetti said your luggage has been delayed but there are clothes in the wardrobe.'

Had she supplied something of her own for Ida to wear?

'Thank you. That's very kind.'

The other woman shook her head. 'Don't thank me. Thank your husband.'

Her husband!

Every cell in her body rejected the idea. After years of separation, she thought of herself as single or as good as.

For four years she'd been Maddy Wickham, a name chosen to hide her should her grandfather search for her.

Yet it wasn't Fausto Calogero on her mind. It was Cesare and why he'd brought her to his home. Was he so desperate for this divorce that he didn't dare let her out of his sight?

She stilled, her hand on the wardrobe door. Had he found someone he wanted to marry? That would explain him taking no chances about getting her signature.

Ida was surprised by the dart of discomfort under her ribs as the idea took root.

She didn't want to be married to him. So why did the thought of him with another woman unsettle her?

She shook her head. She was tired and stressed, imagining things.

Like the way you keep imagining the feel of his arms around you. And how it felt with that gorgeous body pressed up close.

Firming her mouth, she wrenched open the cupboard door, and discovered it wasn't a wardrobe but a room.

Ida paused, dumbfounded as she scanned the bespoke storage running around the large space, the sofa in the centre and the floor-to-ceiling mirror that reflected the image of her wrapped in her plush bath towel.

She blinked. It wasn't the luxury that stole her breath, but the fact it was full of clothes. Clothes in clear plastic as if they'd just come from the cleaners or, she realised as she stepped in and got a proper look, from a couture house.

Dazed, she took in the sight of clothes for every occasion. Shelves that held more shoes than she'd owned in her life, all in her size. Drawers containing underwear of cobweb-fine silk and lace, again in her size.

Icy fingers of warning danced across her scalp and down to her prickling nape.

What had she walked into?

What did Cesare want from her?

Ida breathed deep, tamping down coiling unease. She'd demand answers when she saw him.

But instead of reaching for a pair of jeans or plain tailored trousers, she let her gaze linger on a dress that stood out against the blocks of solid colour. Without intending to she found her hand moving out, lifting the plastic and stroking the fabric.

It was as soft and weightless as she'd suspected. A delicate floral with tiny bunches of dark violets and pale leaves on a creamy background. It had a gathered skirt, a fitted bodice, and a ribbon of dark violet velvet that ran under the bust and up to form narrow shoulder straps.

It was a party dress, delicate and pretty, and it reminded her of the dreams she'd had as a girl. About parties and romance and a bright future.

Ida's hand fell, her mouth compressing. She needed something plain and businesslike. She didn't need…

But suddenly she *did*.

Life had been tough for years, a combination of worry, struggle and drudgery. In London her only clothes were cheap trousers and T-shirts she wore to work, an inadequate coat and a collection of second-hand pullovers she wore at home to counteract the chill when they couldn't afford heating.

Why not wear a pretty dress while she had the

chance? Why not do something just because it made her happy?

Ida felt decadently selfish and daring as she reached for the coat hanger.

Cesare sensed her before he saw her. The air grew charged, crackling with unseen energy.

He didn't like it. That elemental awareness of Ida should have ended years ago, when she'd left him high and dry, a groom without a bride, the cynosure of public speculation and gossip.

He swung around and his breath caught.

Just like that.

One look and the oxygen bled from his lungs while fire combusted in his lower body.

How did a woman who made her living dressed as a cheap hooker manage to look like a breath of spring—delicate, lovely and wholesome? And incredibly alluring.

Was she trying to pretend she didn't work in a sex club by dressing as a sweet innocent?

Amazingly, she almost succeeded, except that his body's avid response told its own story. It recognised the starkly sensual woman beneath the flowers and ribbons.

How long since a woman had made him breathless with wanting?

No one since her.

It seemed incredible. He assured himself it was because he'd been too busy to think about women when he'd had the battle of his life saving the family business.

'Ida.' The name ground low from a throat turned tight with hunger. That hunger, inexplicable and unwanted, prompted him to go on. 'You look completely different. You only wear leather after dark?'

It was a cheap shot that made him almost ashamed. Discomfiting her because she got to him should be beneath him. But apart from a hint of heightened colour along her cheekbones, she betrayed no sign of being discomposed as she entered his study.

'That's a work uniform, not my choice.'

Cesare watched the feathery fabric swirl around her bare legs, took in the way that dark ribbon underscored her breasts, and the gleam of her pale, bare shoulders and arms. Ida was even more devastating than he remembered.

Four years ago she'd rocked him to the core, threatening his focus. Now he faced the fact he'd tried to avoid last night, that she still affected him at the most elemental level.

'Since we're talking about clothes...' She stopped before him and he realised that behind her composure lurked something else. Anxiety? 'Whose dress is this? There's a room full of clothes in my size.'

Cesare scowled, remembering. 'They're yours.'

Now he got a reaction. She started and faltered back. 'I don't understand. You weren't expecting me here.'

'On the contrary, I was. Four years ago.'

'Four years…?' She blinked and surveyed him with dilated pupils. 'After the wedding?'

'Of course, after the wedding.' He shoved his hands into his trouser pockets. 'As my wife you'd attract a lot of attention, more so as I head a luxury goods company. It was important you dress the part, showcasing fashion from our designers. I had my people organise a suitable wardrobe.'

Because, though expensive, the clothes she'd worn before had never seemed quite right on her, despite her poise and grace. They'd looked as if she'd chosen them only for their high price tag, not because they suited her.

'Except you disappeared in the night, leaving me to deal with the furore.'

She lifted one eyebrow. 'Don't expect me to apologise. No woman would have stayed after what you said that night.'

Ida tried to make him out to be at fault? It was she and her grandfather who'd blackmailed *him*.

'If you can't face the truth…'

Her eyes flashed and unholy excitement dug its claws into his belly. The devil in him, the one he kept leashed, responded to that spark of fire. Yet instead of following through she looked away.

When that green gaze met his again, he read no emotion there. 'Why did you keep the clothes, Cesare? You surely didn't want me to return and use them.'

Could she really believe that? Pride demanded he disabuse her of that idea.

'Nothing so puerile. I just forgot about them.'

'Forgot?' She stared as if she didn't understand English. 'A whole *room* of designer clothes?'

This time he was sure her amazement was real. It puzzled him. Whatever her circumstances now, she was heir to a fortune. She'd be used to designer clothes and other luxuries.

'I had other things on my mind. My business. Dealing with your grandfather. Quelling the worst rumours about your disappearance, including the ones that painted me as a Bluebeard who'd done away with his wife.'

Ida's head jerked back. 'You're kidding!'

'You know it's true. Even if the reputable news outlets didn't say it, there was enough gossip.'

It had been horrendous. The only positive the fact that through him the Brunetti brand was constantly in the limelight and doing better than ever.

Her wide-eyed stare bored into his. 'I didn't know. I didn't follow the news.'

Cesare frowned. 'It was splashed across social media.'

She shook her head. 'Not that either.'

It was too unlikely to be true, yet despite his reservations Cesare began to wonder. What had she been doing with her time?

'You really kept a room full of designer clothes for me all this time?'

'If I'd thought about it, I'd have got rid of them. But I forgot until I talked to my housekeeper about getting you more suitable clothes than the ones you arrived in.'

'I see.'

Did she? Cesare didn't want her getting the idea he'd been sentimental about what had been not so much a wedding gift as a necessity so she looked the part as his wife.

'Just as well I hadn't disposed of them.'

The idea of her parading around his home in her raunchy clothes set up a flurry of distaste in his belly.

It *was* distaste, he was sure.

Just over half an hour later Cesare returned to his study after seeing his lawyer out.

He still couldn't believe it. He'd been sure Ida would find some last-minute reason not to agree to a divorce. Yet it had gone smoothly. She'd read the papers, asked a few questions, then signed without hesitation.

He was on the way to becoming a free man.

Exultation rose.

It had taken years to manoeuvre Calogero out of the business and soon he hoped to see the old villain behind bars. Now the unwanted wife Cesare had been blackmailed into accepting had agreed to a divorce without a murmur.

Why would she do that? If she ran true to type,

as venal as her grandfather, she'd make his life difficult while she tried to negotiate a better pay-out.

Cesare had so many questions that needed answering. Plus any inside information he could get about Calogero could only help his cause.

'How do I get to Florence?'

Ida stood near the window, the light creating a fiery nimbus around her bright hair. Sunshine back-lit her, revealing the delectable figure beneath that filmy dress.

Cesare's pulse stalled then sped into overdrive, thundering through his body. He hesitated a second, telling himself it was her unexpected question that threw him, not the desire clawing at him.

He moved into the room. 'Why?'

'To leave, of course. I've signed the papers.'

Ida was full of surprises. Once more she defied expectations. But their business wasn't over.

'Shall we sit and discuss that?' Because he could do without the distraction of seeing her body so lovingly revealed against the light.

After a second, she shrugged and took a chair near the fireplace. Cesare took the one opposite.

'You want to leave?'

She frowned. 'Naturally.'

'And go where? To your flat where your grandfather's man will find you?'

She stiffened. 'That's no concern of yours.'

'It is if you've fallen out with Calogero.'

Or was it his henchman she feared?

Wary eyes held his, but she said nothing.

'Have you, Ida? Have you fallen out with the old man?'

Her lips curved into a crooked smile that snagged something buried deep inside. 'You could say that.'

Then, as quickly as it came, that hint of humour disappeared, leaving her expression strained. Once more Cesare felt that unexpected tug of connection. As he had last night when she'd been scared.

'You could stay here for a short time,' he said slowly, gauging her reaction. 'You'd be safe and I'm guessing you'll need time to plan your next move.'

Instantly a voice sounded in his head.

Remember your father. His poor decisions, his foolishness when in thrall to some woman.

But this was different. Cesare wasn't taken in by Ida. He simply recognised her terror and couldn't ignore it.

Her eyes rounded. 'Why would you do that?'

Because he wasn't an ogre. He didn't like the idea of any woman in fear of a thug.

'Because you're afraid of him.'

Ida said nothing but her stare was eloquent. It was the wary look of a woman who'd seen too much.

Cesare felt a flare of compassion. She'd been part of the scheme to blackmail and control him but, he realised, maybe her own situation had been difficult. He thought of that investigator's report, of a girl orphaned at eight then shuttled between a remote island and Calogero's ostentatious London house.

'But I'm not your responsibility. You hate me.'

Cesare didn't deny it and for reasons Ida refused to examine, that still hurt.

Finally, he spoke. 'You surely didn't expect friendship from a man who was forced with threats to marry you.'

No. But she'd been such an innocent she hadn't realised the situation. She'd imagined Cesare had at least liked her and found her attractive. She smoothed her palms down the delicate fabric of her dress. If he hadn't revealed the truth that night in Rome, if she'd discovered he'd ordered this romantic dream of a dress for her, she might even have tumbled further into—

'No, I don't expect friendship.'

'But things have changed, Ida.'

Her head snapped up and she met that steady dark gaze. 'How?'

'You connived against me, but we could be mutually beneficial to each other now.'

Ida contemplated telling him again that she hadn't been privy to her grandfather's blackmail. That she hadn't been Cesare's enemy. Because it hurt that he should think her to be anything like her grandfather. But he wouldn't believe her. She had no proof, just her word.

'Go on.'

'You've fallen out with your grandfather and so have I. Our interests coincide that far at least. I'll do whatever I can to stop him getting what he wants. If he wants you it will give me great pleasure to deny him that.'

'You're saying you'd keep him away from me just to thwart him?'

Something flashed in Cesare's eyes. An expression she couldn't read, but it made her warier than ever.

'Is that so unlikely?'

It should be. She'd seen Cesare's disdain for her.

Yet last night he'd acted decisively when he understood she was frightened. Surely bringing her all the way to Italy meant there was kindness beneath that steely determination?

Or was he simply another man like her grandfather, determined to win at all costs?

Ida shivered. She couldn't blame Cesare for despising Fausto Calogero. She did too. But she'd seen how the need for revenge blackened a man's soul, eating away any trace of decency.

Yet there was something more. Something she sensed he wasn't telling her.

But what? She didn't know her grandfather's secrets. If Cesare wanted to milk her for information, he'd be disappointed.

She hadn't even seen her grandfather since the wedding, for which she was thankful. The last four years had been a struggle, but in some ways they'd been the happiest of her life, the most free since those halcyon days before the accident when her parents had been alive.

Ida shot to her feet, emotions in such turmoil she couldn't sit still. Doubts crowded her mind and above all the awareness of Cesare, big and predatory.

And fascinatingly male.

'Ida?' His deep voice grazed her skin, drawing it tight and, to her horror, making her nipples bud. Heat stroked through her, down her abdomen to that restless place between her thighs.

'I need time to think.'

She turned away, trying to block him from her thoughts, but it was impossible. Even with him metres away she was hyper-aware of him.

That feeling had burst into life last night the moment she'd looked up to see him before her. But if she was honest the trembling awareness, the desire, had never really gone away. In four years, even telling herself she detested him, the kernel of longing had remained.

Suddenly he wasn't metres away. His breath feathered her hair and down her nape and she felt the heat of his body behind her. 'There's another reason you should stay, Ida.'

'There is? What is it?' She turned, then realised her mistake when she looked up and his expression stole her breath.

Cesare's hands skimmed her bare arms, creating

incendiary trails, up to her shoulders then higher, to cup her face. It didn't occur to her to object. His touch was gentle, barely there, yet Ida felt it like an earthquake shuddering through her.

He moved closer. 'This.'

CHAPTER SEVEN

His DARK EYES looked black now, gleaming with sinful invitation.

Ida canted forward, leaning into him. By the time she realised what she'd done he'd moved closer as if about to wrap his arms around her.

No, no, no!

She couldn't. He couldn't. The misery of his rejection on their wedding night told her not to trust him.

Yet her body had its own ideas. Her legs had shifted apart, a lush, melting feeling throbbing at her core.

Cesare wanted her. She saw it in his eyes, as clearly as before she'd read contempt.

That was new. Cesare desiring her.

She'd grown up a lot in the last four years. Had seen something similar in the eyes of other men, especially in the last two weeks, working at the club. But never had such a look made her feel eager.

Ida drew herself tall, fighting the craving for more than that featherlight touch. For the feel of his mouth on hers, not fleetingly like when he'd brushed his lips over hers in the church, but with passion.

The depth of her need horrified her.

After four years! How could he spark such a powerful response? She'd hoped last night's visceral awareness had been due to shock and would have vanished today.

'You're inviting me to stay for sex?' Her voice choked with throbbing emotion. 'You think because I worked in that club I'm a prostitute, available for—'

Cesare's thumb pressed against her mouth, stopping her words.

'No! This has nothing to do with where you worked. It's about you and me. Nothing else.'

Ida tilted her head back, out of his hold, but for some reason couldn't get her feet to move. Maybe because the way he looked at her made her believe him.

They stood toe to toe, gazes locked, as he lowered his hands to his sides.

'There *is* no you and me. There never was.'

Despite the hopes she'd once harboured.

'Yet the sexual attraction is still there, isn't it, Ida? It hasn't gone.'

She blinked. Had Cesare just implied he'd *desired* her four years ago?

'You feel that thrill in the blood when our eyes lock, don't you?'

To her horror she felt it now. An effervescence running through her whole body, making her more alive than she'd ever been.

'And the quickened breathing like you can't suck in enough air.'

Ida's eyes widened. How did he know? Her chest

did feel too tight, as if she'd run out of oxygen and her breaths turned rapid and shallow to compensate.

'Are your fingers tingling because you want to reach out and touch me?' His voice dropped low. 'Mine are, Ida. I want to touch you. All over.'

She swallowed and clenched her hands, telling herself she didn't feel the same. Refusing to think of Cesare's long fingers stroking her flesh. Stroking places where no man had ever touched, except him in those restless erotic dreams.

She wanted to tell him to stop but feared her voice would betray how he affected her.

'What else are you feeling, Ida? You're flushed. Did you know that? Flushed with desire. Is your pulse thudding hard and fast, down low in your body?'

Snatching in a sharp breath, she finally found the willpower to move. She stepped back, telling herself his persuasive words were just that, they couldn't actually affect her.

Except they had. Ida felt everything he'd said and more. Her pulse drummed hard and fast, and she felt it at her feminine core. At the juncture of her thighs where moisture bloomed.

She might not have been with a man, but Ida understood what that meant.

Why, oh, why did it have to be Cesare Brunetti of all people who turned her on, ripening her body so that all she could think about was how it would feel to surrender to him?

'You have a marvellous imagination, Cesare.' Her voice was husky, so she swallowed and tried again. 'But if you want sex, you need to look elsewhere.'

He shook his head, his eyes never leaving hers, the knowledge in them holding her captive.

'If only things were so simple.' He drew in a breath and her attention snagged on the rise of those powerful shoulders. 'You complicate my life, Ida. *You're* the one I want. Not some nameless woman. *You.*'

Ida stared, dumbfounded, as that needy being inside her leapt into eager life.

He made it sound like no other woman would do. Surely that was admitting to weakness. If she'd learned anything from her grandfather it was not to reveal weakness, especially before your enemy.

How did Cesare view her?

'Careful, Cesare, I might be tempted to think you care.'

He laughed. It was over almost as soon as it started but that deep-throated chuckle scythed through taut muscles and every protective bastion, leaving her adrift.

She liked his laugh, she realised in astonishment. So much that she wanted to hear it again.

Don't go there.

'You're not as I remember you, Ida. You've changed.'

'It would be nice to think that was a compliment,

but you know, Cesare, I don't care what you think of me. I don't like you.'

Once she'd hung on his words and his rare smiles. She'd imagined a future for them that was full of promise. So when he'd turned on her, throwing her grandfather's crimes at her and judging her guilty too, she'd crumpled. Ida was stronger now.

'Liking isn't necessary for what I'm suggesting.' His mouth lifted in a slow smile that, despite her determination to be unaffected, curled her toes and planted heat deep in her body. 'In fact, the tension between us will add spice. You know I'm not suggesting we embark on a meaningful relationship.'

'Oh, I got *that.*' Her tone was as dismissive as she could make it. 'You want sex. I can see it in your eyes.'

'And I can see in your eyes that you do too.'

His voice was soft, like a velvet ribbon trailing across her shivery skin before wrapping around her insides.

'Looks are deceptive.'

It was a blatant lie, but she'd crawl over broken glass before admitting it. Instead, she shrugged and fought the impulse to take another step away. Cesare would see that for what it was, proof that the force field he radiated made her body spark and tingle.

'Anyway, I'm leaving.'

'That's your prerogative. Where will you go that he won't find you? Your grandfather knows now that you left with me. He'll have people keeping an eye on my homes. People who'll follow you once you're out of my protection.'

It made sickening sense. Of course they'd be looking for her. Ida's hope of disappearing among the tourists of Florence before moving on died. She hadn't thought further than that, apart from knowing that she couldn't return to her flat, or to her cousin in Scotland. Both would be under surveillance.

'What are you suggesting, Cesare?' Her hands found her hips and her stare narrowed. 'That you'll keep me and protect me from my grandfather on condition I give you sex?'

His head snapped back and for the first time since they'd met Ida saw she'd rattled him. It lasted barely a moment, so brief that a second later she wondered if she'd imagined his shock.

But it made her feel better to think he abhorred the idea.

Cesare raised both hands and stepped back.

'Calogero might have given me a master class in ruthlessness, but I don't model myself on him. I'm not a blackmailer or rapist.' His chest rose on a mighty breath and Ida saw she'd actually punctured his arrogant air of assurance. 'I've never forced a woman and I'm not going to start now.'

He paused, staring down at her from under lowered brows as if to make sure his words sank in.

'As for letting you stay here safely while you make your plans, that offer stands, no strings attached.'

Ida saw the truth in his face. It was a genuine offer.

'I… Thank you.'

Once again she realised how much she owed him. He'd spirited her out of London to safety when he could simply have waited for her signature on his papers then left her to manage. Now he offered to extend that protection until she worked out her escape plan.

His generosity puzzled her. And made her feel wobbly. It was easier to deal with this man when she could simply hate him.

'As for pursuing this attraction, we're both adults, and neither of us is under any illusions that this is more than sexual. All I'm saying is that in the middle of this fiasco your grandfather tangled us in, we could take some pleasure for ourselves. Nothing more, nothing less.'

'Because it's convenient?' She hoped her tone sounded sardonic rather than hurt.

'You think any of this is *convenient*?'

His eyes flashed and once again it seemed she'd pushed him into uncharted territory. That was exactly what he did to her. Then his expression shuttered.

'But you're right. The fact we're divorcing only makes it better. No chance of confusion about this meaning more than it does. We can enjoy a short affair and get this,' he gestured wide in a way that looked wholly Italian, 'attraction out of our systems before moving on to separate lives.'

'Like scratching an itch?'

He inclined his head. 'Exactly.'

Perhaps Ida was naïve but the sensations bombarding her when she was with Cesare felt far more complicated than an itch.

What did she know? She'd never had an affair, casual or otherwise.

Maybe he was right. If they had sex maybe her fascination for him might finally fade.

And maybe that was dangerous temptation talking.

'We're in a unique position,' he continued. 'Married and on the brink of divorce but never had a wedding night.' His eyes locked on hers and she had to fight not to shift her weight because parts of her anatomy responded far too emphatically to that stare. 'Maybe that's the problem. We never gave our attraction its natural outlet.'

'A wedding night?' She shook her head, but the movement felt stiff. 'As I recall, you didn't want sex. You were in a foul mood.'

'Can you blame me?'

No. She'd understood his anger. Her grandfather had targeted a proud man and brought him almost to his knees. No wonder Cesare had been furious.

But that was no excuse for attacking her. She'd been a victim of the old man's machinations too. Not that she could prove it, and she knew Cesare wouldn't take her word for it, not after his experiences with her family.

'You behaved appallingly,' she said finally.

She saw he hadn't expected her to call him out on that. But then *he* surprised *her.* 'I did. I'd kept everything under control for so long and suddenly it all came rushing out. I didn't mean to drive you away. Most of my anger was directed at your grandfather.'

Most, not all. And that wasn't a proper apology. Yet it was closer than she'd ever expected to get.

'That's no excuse.'

'True. I pride myself on keeping an even temper and not responding to provocation. But that night…' He shook his head. 'Anger and thwarted sexual attraction are a dangerous mix.'

Thwarted attraction? He'd wanted her that night?

It shouldn't colour her thinking yet the primitive part of Ida yearning for Cesare's touch swelled in triumph. It didn't negate his behaviour, but it was a tiny salve to her pride.

'You think sharing a belated wedding night will help you move on?' She tried to sound cynical but feared her husky voice told a different story.

'Help *us*, Ida. This is mutual. You know it is.'

She looked away, not liking the stirring in her blood. 'It's an interesting idea. I'll give it some thought.'

'Just so we're absolutely clear, I won't ask again.' She felt her eyes widen and turned back to him. 'I won't pressure you. You're not obliged to sleep with me for my protection.' On the words *sleep with me* his eyelids drooped, giving his eyes a lazy, suggestive gleam that made her stomach twist in eager corkscrews. 'The choice of when we get together will be entirely yours.'

When not *if*?

He had the arrogance of the devil. Indignation stirred. As if she'd give herself to a man so self-satisfied!

Something flickered in his expression. Amusement? Impatience?

She was on the point of leaving the room when a thought hit her. Something more important than Cesare's ego and sense of entitlement.

'I'm glad to hear you're willing to wait.' Her tone told him he could wait till hell froze over and she let a smug smile curl her mouth. 'In the meantime, I need to send something to London. Is there a local post office?'

Not that she really wanted to venture out if Bruno or someone like him was lurking in the vicinity.

'Can't you send a text or email?'

'It's not a message, it's a parcel.'

Cesare's eyes narrowed in suspicion. 'You didn't bring any luggage.'

Did he think she'd swiped one of the precious pieces of art from upstairs and hoped to post it under his nose? Ida would have smiled if she weren't tired of his suspicions. Instead she felt it like a blade to her heart.

How could this man do that to her? He'd always made her feel too much.

Her hands found her hips and her chin hiked up. 'I need to send Jo the clothes and shoes I wore last night.'

'Jo, your flatmate?'

Ida nodded. Still he didn't give her the information she needed. Was there a postal outlet here or did she have to organise a courier? That would cost more but Jo needed her gear, something Ida hadn't considered last night when she'd let Cesare usher her onto a flight to Italy. All she'd cared about was escaping Bruno.

'Why?'

Damn the man for being so intractable and curious. For four years he hadn't thought about her and now he seemed determined to dig through her life.

Instinctive reticence warred with Ida's need to do the right thing by her friend.

'They're Jo's clothes, okay? I borrowed them so I could work her shifts at the club, but she needs them back.' Jo was on a tight budget and couldn't spare the cash to replace them, especially that leather bustier.

Ida had the satisfaction of seeing Cesare stare as if for once robbed of words. It didn't last long.

'Why would you want to do that?'

Ida turned away, folding her arms across her body as she stared out at the spectacular view of undulating hills. A line of dark cypress trees marked a road or boundary, and in the distance a small hilltop town looked picturesque and inviting. The scene was a mix of gentle greens and ochres under the clear blue sky and she wished she could absorb some of its glorious tranquillity.

'Jo got mugged.' She shivered, remembering the trip to the emergency department and the fear that her friend's injuries might be more severe than just bruises. 'She wasn't well enough to work at first. Even when she improved, she couldn't work behind the bar because make-up couldn't hide those bruises.'

'You took her place?' Cesare's tone held a spiky note she didn't bother to analyse.

'For two weeks. Jo couldn't afford to lose the job. She goes back next week.'

'I thought you said you had your own job.'

'I do.'

Ida chewed her lip, thinking of the customer base she'd built up through hard work, and the efforts she and Jo had made to retain that. Ida had worked all hours between the bar and her cleaning jobs, trying to juggle everything. Jo had pitched in when she was well enough, taking over some of Ida's night shift office-cleaning, which was why Ida hadn't expected her at home last night.

Yet even if Ida returned to London it would need to be to a completely different area if she wanted to stay under the radar. She'd have to give up her clients and start from scratch.

'Ida?'

Cesare regarded her with a curious look on his face, one she couldn't identify. 'You were only working there while your friend was sick?'

It was none of his business, but she was tired of shoring up the barriers between them.

'For a fortnight. Last night was my last shift and she'll go back in two days. Do you know how long the mail will take?'

He stared at her as if puzzling something out. But what was there to puzzle? He'd made up his mind about her character years before.

Unless he intended to rescind his suggestion for an affair? Maybe the fact she'd worked in the bar *had* prompted the suggestion after all.

Ida's pulse quickened, not in excitement but, to her amazement, with nerves. As if she didn't want him to change his mind. She took her time digesting that.

Instead of being outraged at Cesare's proposition she felt intrigued.

Tempted.

'Forget the mail,' he said brusquely. 'Give it all to Dorotea to package up and I'll have it delivered.'

'I'll write out the address and—'

'I have it.'

Ida frowned. He sounded out of sorts, grumpier than before, though why that should be she had no idea.

'Great. Thanks. I'll get them.'

Cesare shoved his hands in his trouser pockets and watched her go, trying to tamp down his wholly masculine response to her gently swaying hips and the swish of that skirt around her bare legs. The pearlescent gleam of her bare shoulders and the combination of bright, upswept hair revealing a slender neck drove a punch of longing into his gut.

His jaw firmed. It didn't matter what she looked like. She was still the woman who'd helped blackmail him for his money and connections.

Except she hasn't tried to get anything from you in years.

Only because she had Calogero to fall back on until they fell out. And the prospect of a healthy divorce settlement to look forward to.

Cesare dragged his hands from his pockets and opened the French doors, needing fresh air. He stepped outside, breathing in the scents of sunshine on old stonework and freshly mown grass. Of all the exquisite, expensive perfumes his luxury goods company produced, none compared to the scent of home. This place grounded him.

To think he'd almost lost it, along with everything his family had worked for, because of Calogero.

Yet it wasn't relief he felt. His emotions were in turmoil, buffeted by Ida's revelations.

Her fear of her grandfather's henchman evoked sympathy. The way she'd stood up to Cesare appealed too, even as it frustrated him. It felt like drawing blood from a stone, getting information from her.

Why would she want to share with you? She doesn't like you. Just as you don't like her.

And yet…

Cesare frowned as he moved into the garden, feeling the sun's warmth. He tipped up his head. After the miserable cold in London this felt glorious.

Except for the churning in his belly. The knowledge he'd jumped to at least one mistaken conclusion about his soon-to-be ex-wife.

It shouldn't matter that she'd only worked in that strip club to help a friend. It wasn't his business how she earned a living. A woman could choose where she worked.

So why had he almost exploded with fury when he'd found her there, just as his investigators had said? Why had he been determined to drag her out? And why had he teetered on the brink of violence when he saw men eyeing her like a delicacy they wanted to devour?

Sex. That was why. He wanted her. Badly. The fact he'd lusted after her while she flaunted herself like that had infuriated him.

But why?

She was his wife on paper only. She had no place in his life.

For some reason seeing her in that place had taken him to the brink of civilised behaviour. Discovering she'd been there as a favour to a friend filled him with a relief he had no right to feel, as well as admiration for the way she helped her injured friend.

Now she seemed almost as concerned about returning those clothes as she was about her own predicament.

Ida Montrose—no, Ida Brunetti for the moment—was more complex than he'd imagined. She was doing his head in.

The fact she was a loyal friend and that she'd broken with Calogero didn't negate the way she'd made him a laughing stock, first with the blackmail and then her disappearance.

The fact he wanted her body had nothing to do with any of that.

Yet he was mired in questions, not just about Ida but also about his responses to her. Surely lust and the prospect of a brief affair didn't require so much soul-searching.

But if, in the course of their affair, he was to discover information that would help bring down Calogero faster, so much the better.

Ida might be wary. She might not like him. But, despite her words and frosty looks, she was rubbish at concealing that she wanted him as much as he wanted her.

A warm glow settled in his belly.

Satisfaction. And anticipation.

CHAPTER EIGHT

IDA STOOD ON the long balcony outside her bedroom. The sun had set but there was enough light to see the undulating countryside. Here and there were pinpricks of light from a far-off farmhouse or, on a distant hill, a town.

After London's chill the air felt balmy. Floral scents perfumed the night.

What would it be like living in a place like this? A place both beautiful and abundant. She'd grown to appreciate the extremes of the tiny island where she'd been raised. The white beaches and aquamarine but icy water, the brisk wind that turned so easily into a lashing gale that made you glad to be snug indoors.

Through the recent years in London she'd longed for the countryside. A quiet village rather than the bustle of the city. A place that felt like home, not just a refuge from the dangerous city streets.

She needed to decide on a place to start again. Should she try Liverpool or Birmingham? Somewhere big so she could lose herself in the crowd?

But that hadn't protected her from her grandfather or Cesare. They'd found her eventually.

Should she try for a smaller market town, even a village? But she had to work. Maybe a town.

She supposed it was possible she'd get some

money on her divorce, but most likely her grandfather had manipulated the prenuptial contract so it would be channelled via him. Besides, she wasn't sure she wanted Cesare's money, not after what her family had done to him.

Frustrated, she leaned on the balustrade. It was tranquil and, despite its being Cesare's house, she felt at peace. Maybe it was the quiet. Or the fact he'd left her alone to think. Knowing she was safe, even if her grandfather had guessed her location, made a huge difference.

Yet despite the serenity, Ida couldn't relax.

Because of Cesare's suggestion that they share the wedding night they'd never had.

He had a nerve!

But indignation was no match for other feelings. Fascination. Desire. Temptation.

She was twenty-three and she'd never been with a man.

Apart from those miserable months staying with her grandfather, she'd spent most of her life on a small island. She'd been home-schooled by Kate, her mother's cousin, and later via online courses.

She'd had little to do with men, except for her dreadful grandfather.

Ida had told herself she'd fallen for Cesare's looks and charisma because she was inexperienced. Yet in four years she hadn't wanted a sexual experience with any other man.

From the moment he'd erupted back into her

world she'd been fixated on him. Beneath every interaction was the sizzle of awareness. Even now she felt the shivery run of nerves under her skin.

She didn't like him. Yet there was something between them she couldn't deny.

Was it just sexual attraction? She hoped so, given the dangerous romantic dreams she'd woven about him before. It would be a relief if this was simple chemistry that could be eradicated by a fling.

He knew what he was talking about. He must have had lots of lovers.

Yet to give herself to him…

Ida didn't like putting herself in any man's power. Surely if they had sex, she'd be vulnerable to him?

But he'd admitted to vulnerability too. He'd said he wanted her in Rome.

Ida straightened and turned to walk the length of the long balcony, too keyed up to stay still.

Two things puzzled her: Cesare's kindness, for it *was* kindness, spiriting her away from Bruno, and his confession that he was drawn to her.

Had Cesare altered or just revealed what he'd hidden before?

The man was an enigma. He bothered and teased and fascinated her—

'Can't sleep, Ida?'

The velvety rumble stopped her in her tracks.

Slowly she turned. French doors stood open into a bedroom and a familiar tall figure stood propped against the door jamb.

Her pulse jumped.

Ida couldn't read Cesare's expression. But one glance absorbed his air of lazy masculine power, of intensity beneath the casual stance. His arms were crossed over his bare chest.

A surge of white noise in her ears blanked out the night as she took in that expanse of naked flesh, from straight shoulders all the way down to the narrow girth at his hips where he still wore trousers. His crossed arms emphasised his strength.

She'd sensed it when he was fully clothed but seeing him revealed now, albeit in the shadows, took her breath.

Ida grabbed the balustrade, stone biting her fingers.

'Cesare! I didn't realise…' She wouldn't have walked the length of the balcony if she'd known it led to the master suite.

Would she?

'That's disappointing.' Ida couldn't read his tone. Not amusement but something that she felt as a trickle of heat under her skin. 'I thought you'd decided to join me.'

With the light behind him it was impossible to read Cesare's expression, yet his body told its own tale. He might look relaxed, but the set of his shoulders belied that. As did the tension emanating from him.

Was his heart beating as fast as hers?

Ida wanted to plant her hand on his chest. A tingle ran across her palm as she imagined how it would feel. Would his chest hair be silky soft or crisp?

She swallowed, hands clenching to resist the temptation of him.

'I was just pacing while I make some plans.'

'Ah.' Cesare straightened. 'There was I imagining you thinking about us.'

Ida was about to say there was no *us* but stopped. Why protest when he was right?

Life had taught her to face problems. Pretending they didn't exist never worked. This *was* a problem. For years Cesare had been there, a weakness she couldn't expunge. Distance hadn't helped, nor had hatred, distress or abstinence.

She drew a breath that felt like a sob.

She'd *tried* to resist him, but it wasn't working. What would it take to be free of this man?

Years of abstinence hadn't cured her. Was it possible his crazy proposition might?

Ida's gaze traced his powerful body. How would it feel to touch him? To stroke him all over, learn the sensations of his body against hers? Discover...?

Was that what this was? A desperation to discover sex?

She'd never had the opportunity for sexual experimentation earlier, and lately she'd been too busy surviving. Perhaps *that* was why now she felt so driven. Ida drew a relieved breath. That was much less scary than the idea that there was something special about Cesare Brunetti.

She should be thinking about transport, accommodation and work. Instead her mind buzzed with awareness of *him*.

Nothing was certain in this life, especially happiness. Joy was rare and fleeting. Maybe it wasn't joy she felt at the prospect of being with him, but it was compelling and as far away from fear as she could get.

Without letting herself think, she walked up to Cesare. He didn't stop her, simply unfolded his arms to give her free access as she planted her hands on his chest.

Excitement shivered through her as she got her answer. Surprisingly soft hair, not coarse, over hot, silky skin and hard muscle. She spread her fingers, splaying her hands, relishing each new sensation.

Cesare's heart thudded beneath her palm, steady but fast.

That pleased her and gave her the confidence to lean in and nuzzle the broad slope of his chest. She pressed her lips there, darted out the tip of her tongue and tasted something new. The dark, sultry tang of Cesare Brunetti.

A shudder racked her from the back of her skull to her toes and everywhere in between.

She'd thought she knew longing. Now she realised how much she had to learn. She'd just opened a Pandora's box of desire. And she wanted more.

Cesare watched Ida stalk across the balcony like a warrior going into battle. Would she argue or even slap him for his provocation?

Nothing prepared him for the impact of her hands across his flesh or the shock of her mouth on him.

His head ricocheted back, his breath an urgent gasp as she seduced him with lips and tongue and the possessive swipe of her exploring hands.

His arms came around her, holding her to him just in case she had any thoughts about retreating.

He doubted she even noticed. She was rubbing her face against him and over the rush of blood in his ears he caught the tiniest sound. Something between a growl and a purr. It came from Ida.

His nostrils flared as his body responded to that innately sexy sound. He planted his feet wide, drawing her against him.

He'd hoped she'd come to him because she wanted him but hadn't truly believed it. Nothing in life was so simple. Especially not his wife.

Cesare stiffened, a jolt of pure hunger driving through his groin as teeth scraped near his collarbone.

'Ida.' He didn't know if it was a warning or a groan of delight. All he knew was that he needed more.

He cradled her cheeks, gently tilting her face up. He saw the gleam of slitted eyes and darkened lips, still open from where she'd nibbled his skin.

Cesare lowered his head, waiting for her response. Could this be a tease? A taunt to bring him to his knees while she demanded some additional divorce settlement?

Once more Ida cut through old expectations with devastating simplicity. She swayed closer, her breasts in that pretty dress against his bare torso, her hips nestling against his groin.

Triumph melded with need and, yes, desperation, turning his body to unyielding hardness. But as he bent his head, inhaling Ida's fresh spring scent, his touch was gentle. Their lips met and clung and Cesare felt his hands tremble. As if he'd waited so long for this that he couldn't believe it was real.

Her cheeks were soft, her lips too. That made him leash the hammering urge to take her quickly. Instead he wanted to savour every sensation.

Savour Ida.

He swiped his tongue across her open lips then delved further, fascinated by the quick clench of her fingertips where they clung now to his upper arms. Then she relaxed, leaning against him as her tongue briefly touched his.

It was crazy but Cesare felt that brief connection like a thunderbolt passing through his body. He tingled all over as if from an electric shock.

He angled his head for better access, exploring her mouth, losing himself in lush sweetness that tasted faintly of cherries. Their tongues met again, not a darting foray this time but a sliding caress. His eyes closed as, stunned, he registered the extent of his arousal. Just from a kiss!

Ida's hands crept up his shoulders, around his neck and into his hair, tugging him to the edge of pain. The sting only made his senses spark as he deepened their kiss. It was the most flagrantly erotic yet strangely innocent kiss he could remember.

It took him to the edge in seconds. Four years of celibacy took their toll. That had to be the reason this felt like nothing he'd ever experienced.

Cesare dragged air through his nostrils, seeking control. Then Ida rose on her toes, her breasts pushing against his chest as she kissed him deeply.

Thought crumbled beneath that ardent onslaught. Cesare dropped his hands to her hips, holding her high against him, giving back kiss for kiss till he heard it again, that tiny purr of pleasure from the back of her throat.

It galvanised him. Firming his hold, he swung her round and settled her back against the door jamb, stepping in close so she didn't slide down to the floor. Her hands tightened in his hair and then he was helping her lift her legs around his hips.

His hands met soft layers of fabric then smooth, cool skin, and fire ignited.

'Ida.' Her name was a gravel growl in his throat and lower, in his belly where the need for her had been building for so long.

'Cesare.'

Did he hear it or just feel the vibration of her assent through their locked mouths? Either way, nothing had ever sounded so good.

Sweat broke out at the back of his neck as he lifted his hands, dragging them up her slender frame to cup her breasts. They fitted his hands perfectly and, though he longed to tear her free of the fabric, he restrained himself.

Cesare settled for massaging her breasts, finding her nipples through the flimsy fabric and rolling them between his fingers, feeling her body jerk in response and her pelvis thrust towards him.

He lifted his mouth, ignoring her protest, to nuzzle her throat, kissing and nipping and hearing her sighs turn to moans that drove the ache of desire to sharp pain.

His groin felt as if it were in a vice. That one wrong move would undo him.

Cesare shut his eyes and drew a deep breath filled with hyacinths, the rich perfume of warm woman and the beckoning, indefinable scent of arousal.

'I want you, Ida. I need you.'

There was no thought of hiding the truth. Or the fact she'd once been his enemy.

Nothing mattered but *this*.

'Yes, please.'

Please? As if she sought a favour!

His lips curved against her fragrant skin. This would be a mutual favour.

'Hold tight,' he murmured, sliding his arms around her narrow waist and straightening.

It was hard to think when Ida clung to him, when her delicious heat was pressed against his erection. But higher levels of thought weren't required. His body knew what to do, hold her tight and get to his bed as soon as possible. He was barely aware of crossing the threshold but suddenly he was by the bed, illuminated by a single lamp. He turned so that when they fell to the mattress she was on top.

Cesare's eyes shut for a second as he absorbed every detail of delicious sensation.

When he opened them she'd pulled back just enough to look down at him, though their bodies were still plastered together. Desire throbbed through him, and he saw her eyes widen at the twitch of his erection.

That soft green gaze was bewitching. It took a second for him to realise her fixed stare didn't match the message of her eager body.

'What is it?'

'Nothing.' Her pupils dilated as if in surprise. Then she frowned. 'But you need to know I'm not… experienced. I'd rather we went slow.'

Slow? After she'd rocked his world? Her mouth on his flesh, her hands in his hair, her kiss…

And what did she mean by not experienced? He discounted the idea she was a virgin. She'd sashayed up to him with all the confidence of a woman who knew exactly what she wanted.

Maybe she feared he wouldn't take enough time to please her as well as himself. Cesare was about to tell her she didn't need to pretend to innocence. He had every intention of ensuring they both enjoyed this to the full. But he had better things to do than talk.

'I can do slow.' His voice dropped. 'All the better to savour you.'

He watched, fascinated, as colour darkened her cheekbones. And just like that, despite the urgency humming in his blood, *slow* was exactly what he wanted.

CHAPTER NINE

CESARE'S EYES LOOKED almost black, and Ida had no difficulty reading their expression. Anticipation. And something knowing and heated that might have worried her yet instead made her shift against him.

Maybe he hadn't understood. Maybe he didn't realise not experienced meant *no* experience.

But she liked Cesare's heavy-lidded look too much to explain. The last thing she wanted was him changing his mind. If he was happy to go slow, what more could she ask?

Everything about Cesare, from his response to her touch, to his kisses, to the way he'd held her and how his big, bold body felt beneath her right now, confirmed this was exactly what she wanted.

What she needed.

'Aren't you going to kiss me?'

His voice rumbled up from that broad chest beneath her, fascinating her and making her even keener to explore him. She wanted to stroke his firm flesh all over, learn the contours of his body, taste him.

Of course she kissed him again. His kisses were addictive. If she'd known before that a kiss could feel like this…

Ida wondered what he'd say if she revealed she'd never kissed any man but him. But then she was leaning down, lips against his, her tongue reaching out to meet his as he'd taught her, and her mind blanked.

It was the most luscious, decadent thing, lying over Cesare, pressed against his arousal, knowing it was for her.

Her eyes fluttered shut as she gave herself up to a new world of bliss.

Some time later she frowned, belatedly registering something had changed. Even then it took a while to understand her back was on the bed and Cesare was pressed down on her. She gasped against his mouth, wondering at how good that felt.

'Too heavy?' He propped himself up on one elbow, dark hair falling across his brow.

'No.'

But it was too late, he was rolling off her onto his hip. His index finger followed the ribbon running beneath her breasts. His gaze held hers as he traced it up to her shoulder.

'Pretty. So pretty I don't want to tear it. Where's the zip, Ida?'

Something caught in her chest at the idea of Cesare tearing the dress in his urgency. Her pulse thudded once, hard, then she reached for her side.

His hand covered hers. 'Let me.'

Ida lay back and watched him lean over, his hand skimming downwards. The zip sounded incredibly loud then warm fingers touched her hip, her waist, trawling higher.

'So pretty,' he murmured again, as he slipped a finger under first one velvet shoulder strap then another, drawing them down her arms.

But he wasn't looking at the dress. He was staring at her. Then his mouth was on her shoulder, and she was arching towards him.

Cesare's kisses were unhurried and thorough. He moved to her collarbone, to the upper slopes of her breasts and across to her other shoulder, where he nipped at the curve of her neck. Ida's bones turned to liquid.

Her eyes were closed when he pulled back and it took a moment to realise he'd drawn her dress down to her waist. A gentle tug made her lift her hips then she felt the swish of fabric against bare skin as he dragged it off her completely.

Her eyes snapped open. Cesare was surveying her with a curiously shuttered expression. But the throbbing pulse at his temple belied his stillness.

Ida wore a strapless bra and knickers of matching ivory lace. She told herself they were no more revealing than a bikini but the fierce gleam in his eyes told another story. To her surprised delight, she revelled in Cesare's response.

He said something fervent in Italian that curled around her like smoke, feathering her skin and making her shift as an insistent pulse beat between her legs.

'Your turn.'

But he shook his head. 'Not yet. Not if you want us to go slow.'

The way she felt she wasn't sure that slow was an option any longer. But before she could voice that, Cesare lay down beside her and the feel of his hot, bare torso against her stole her breath.

As did his zephyr-light touch, skimming the top of her bra from one side to another, back and forth and back again, making her want more. One finger dipped below the edge of the fabric, sliding across her breast. Her jaw gritted at his teasing and she reached down, towards his belt, only to falter when Cesare pulled the bra cup down and buried his face at her breast.

Was that high, keening note from her? Ida rose off the bed, her hands buried in his hair as she held him to her, afraid he'd stop.

The sensations were incredible. First that exploratory flick of his tongue that shot lightning through her and now… He drew on her breast and it simultaneously pulled her whole body taut yet made a vital part of her melt.

Nothing had ever felt like this. As if he tapped into a vein of raw need.

She slid against him, rocking her hips, needing to feel him against all of her. Then through the haze of wonder came something new: Cesare's hand slipping deftly under the lace at her hips. There was no hesitation, just an arrow-straight dip straight to the hidden cleft where…

'Cesare!'

She shuddered as hot, bright sensation arced between her breast and his questing fingers.

She'd expected this to be good, but she hadn't *known*.

Ida snapped her eyes open and there was Cesare, his mouth locked around her nipple, his black-as-night eyes hot with passion as he circled then pressed just at the place where sensation centred.

Again Ida lifted off the bed. Lightning forked inside her and she hovered, strung out on a peak of incredible ecstasy until, in a blast of blinding delight, everything else fell away.

The only thing anchoring her to reality was Cesare. The warm weight of him solid and reassuring against her as she soared in a sky full of shattering stars.

Finally Ida became aware of the sound of panting. Swift, shallow breaths and the hard pump of her overworked lungs. She trembled all over. Surely her bones had disintegrated in that white-hot light?

Cesare kissed her breast, a tiny caress, but to her overwrought senses it was too much. She shuddered, echoes of bliss still coursing through her.

Did he understand? The next thing she knew he was lying full length beside her, his arm around her shoulder, holding her close to his collarbone, his other hand rubbing gently between her shoulder blades.

Ida sank into him, trying not to feel overwrought by the roaring rush of ecstasy that had engulfed her.

Would it have felt the same with any other man?

Stupid question when she'd never had the least desire to let any man but Cesare this close.

It dawned on her maybe this whole experience was a dreadful mistake.

Too late now. No time for regrets.

Ida's mouth curved against hot, salty skin. Even reeling from her first sexual experience with a man, she realised that thought was solely so she'd stop worrying and lose herself in what Cesare had to offer.

And he had a lot!

Ida had wanted to explore his body and now he let her, with the proviso that his trousers stayed on and she only touched bare flesh.

She was fascinated by his hands, the sweeping indent of his back, the wide sprawl of his shoulders, and the way he jumped when she rolled him over then sat astride him and nipped tiny scraping kisses down his neck.

He was sensitive just below the shoulder blades, and just above his hip. Ida felt a tiny tremor of response when she kissed him there. Heard his hissed breath when she kissed her way down his chest, her hair trailing over him. She was fascinated by the counterpoint of hot, satiny skin and that smattering of hair that felt so good to the touch. How would it feel against her bare breasts?

This was her opportunity to find out. Tonight, the wedding night they'd never had, she could do what she wanted, secure in the knowledge she could walk away tomorrow and never look back.

A sharp pang sheared through her, making her pause.

'Ida? Is something wrong?'

She slanted a look at Cesare, lying with his hands behind his head, biceps curled in a way that created another tight curl, this time in her pelvis. A sexual response, she assured herself, but something more too. *That* disturbed her.

This was supposed to be a fleeting thing, a chance to satisfy and finally eradicate that edgy feeling of need.

'What could be wrong?'

Ida had been alone so long, depending on no one but herself. This yearning for connection rocked her.

Of all the people in the world, Cesare was the last to want more from her than a single night. She couldn't let her mind stray to impossibilities.

She'd make the most of tonight then move on. There was no other option.

'I can't imagine,' he said and reached out, pulling her to him. He held her for a long moment, liquid dark eyes intent on her. 'You would tell me if there's a problem.'

It was neither a question nor a statement. A command perhaps. There *was* something intrinsically commanding about him, even half-dressed. Especially half-dressed, for there was no mistaking his strength and aura of certainty.

Ida envied him. For years she'd felt weak and worried.

But she didn't feel that way as he flicked her bra undone.

She barely had time to realise what he'd done when his hands and mouth were on her and that glorious conflagration started again, fed by his outrageously extravagant praise.

After that, things blurred again. Another swipe of his hands and her underwear was completely gone. Then Cesare set about exploring her even more thoroughly than she had him.

This man had a sixth sense where her body was concerned. He knew, or quickly discovered, where to touch to make her breath catch and her body burn.

By the time he drew back, reaching for the buckle of his belt, Ida was spent, sprawled boneless on the bed, her body shimmering with pleasure after another exquisite climax.

Even so, the sight of Cesare tugging at his belt then rising and pushing the last of his clothes to the floor made every hormone sit up and take note. Watching him roll on a condom was unbelievably arousing, even for a woman who should be comatose from bliss.

The man was beautiful. His body all symmetry and entrancing planes. Ida's gaze dropped to those heavy thighs and above them a spear of an erection that looked potently impressive.

She thought of their difference in size and about scary stories she'd heard of disastrous first times.

Then Cesare's mouth quirked up at one side, probably because of how she stared, and her tremble of nerves subsided. Theirs might be a temporary alliance, but he'd proven patient and considerate.

Remarkable as it was, *she trusted him.*

Ida met his smile with one of her own and lay back, waiting.

That smile. That body.

Did Ida have any idea how she tested his control, lying there looking so tempting? So outrageously seductive and adorably rumpled?

Adorably? Surely not. Yet there was something about her mix of enthusiasm and almost unconscious allure that made him feel protective as well as aroused.

Taking this slow *had* been the best way. Yet now his capacity for delay was gone. Being with Ida each time she came had only made his own need more desperate.

Cesare nudged her knees wide. Her smile disappeared but she lifted her arms, inviting him down to her, and he couldn't stifle the siren's call any longer.

Her body was soft and accommodating, fragrant and welcoming, and he fitted between her hips as if they were made for each other.

He lifted himself on his elbows, not wanting to squash her, but that left his chest just far enough from hers that her peaked nipples teased him with each breath.

Cesare gritted his jaw, feeling the welded-tight pressure in his groin and thighs, the building heat, and knew he wouldn't last.

Her eyes really were the most amazing colour. They beckoned him to Paradise.

Slipping his palm under her thigh, he raised it so her leg was bent, his aim to make it easier for her to take him. She lifted her other leg and even that slide of silky skin felt far, far too good.

Cesare pushed home.

It was all he'd anticipated and more. Much more. Ida fitted him like a velvet glove, so close he had to shut his eyes and concentrate on not losing himself on the first thrust.

But there was more. A snag. An unexpected sensation that made him try to pause, but it was too late. Even as he registered the sensation it was gone.

He opened his eyes and looked down to find Ida wincing, her eyes screwed tight and…was that perspiration on her brow?

His brain conjured an unthinkable possibility.

Was it possible she'd been innocent as in totally inexperienced?

He was still striving to process that when green eyes met his. They looked foggy. With pain?

He was withdrawing, his mind whirling, when

she grabbed his shoulders and pulled. As if she had the strength to stop him going.

No, it was the determined set of her jaw and the way she hitched first one leg higher around his waist, then the other, that stopped him.

'Don't go now.' Her voice had an unfamiliar raspy edge. 'You promised me a wedding night and I want it all.'

Cesare stared into her flushed face, wondering how badly he'd hurt her. Was she saying that because she felt she owed him or because she really wanted this?

'Don't make me plead, Cesare.'

'I wouldn't dream of it.'

He lifted his hand to her cheek, watched her turn and press a kiss to his palm and felt the tight band around his chest ease. He trailed unsteady fingers to her berry-tipped breast and felt it peak as her pupils dilated and her flush deepened.

Slowly Cesare leaned forward, taking her mouth as his body took hers, gently but steadily, aiming to stir her senses as surely as she stirred his.

But his own arousal was too acute for patience. He slipped his hand between them, teasing her with his fingers while he drove into her with all the control he could muster.

Urgent hands grabbed his shoulders then his skull, and to his relief soon he heard the muffled sound of her ecstasy building, felt her little shudders. If he could just last a little longer…

Cesare moved faster, driven by his own rhythm of need, growing more urgent with each thrust. Then he was swallowing her screams of completion and that shot him over the edge, spilling himself in a desperate, pulsating climax that blanked his mind and undid his body in a cataclysm of pleasure.

Rapture was the word that came to his befuddled brain much later as they lay together, he on his back with his arms around her, she with her head buried in his neck. He'd always enjoyed sex but that had reached an entirely new level.

Now and then, another little tremor ran through him, and he'd feel her quiver around him in response. Even that felt too acute, too profound.

Four years of abstinence, he told himself when his head finally cleared. That was the explanation. Four years without a woman in his bed. That was why this seemed phenomenal.

In that time his sole focus had been turning the company around from the disasters after his father took over as CEO when Cesare's grandfather died. That and triumphing over Calogero.

Plus, whether from the old-fashioned values instilled by his grandfather, or from stubborn pride, Cesare hadn't wanted to break his vow of fidelity, even to a wife he didn't respect.

And now? She wouldn't be his wife much longer, which was a relief. Yet he was learning she wasn't as he'd imagined her. Not totally at any rate.

He'd jumped to at least one wrong conclusion about Ida. Was it possible there were others?

The idea disturbed him.

Carefully he withdrew from her, settling her on her side and getting to his feet.

For a full minute he stood, watching her. Her eyes were closed and her mouth slightly open as she slept.

She looked delicate, arousing another burst of protectiveness. She also looked exhausted. Not surprising since it seemed she'd never done this before.

Cesare spied a red mark on her breast and another at her throat and lifted his hand to his jaw, finding it ready for a shave. He felt a spiralling drop in his belly. Guilt that he'd grazed her sensitive skin.

He did *not* experience a secret burst of delight and possessiveness at the idea he was her first lover. Or that she carried the mark of his body on hers.

That would be beneath him. It would be uncivilised.

But hadn't Ida always tapped into a vein of something in him that wasn't sophisticated or enlightened? Right from the beginning he'd responded to her with unvarnished emotions that threatened to cloud his judgement.

The fact she'd taken *him* as her first lover stunned, perplexed and delighted him.

Cesare spun away and headed for the bathroom.

When Ida had appeared on the balcony all he'd been able to think about was how much he wanted her. He'd been wrong to think one brief taste would be enough to satisfy a craving that had built for so long. Especially now.

Even satiated he wanted her.

He had more questions than ever. And he was determined to get answers.

CHAPTER TEN

'I KNOW YOU'RE AWAKE, IDA.'

Ida sighed and burrowed into the pillow. Couldn't he leave her be? He'd got up then stood watching her, and she'd felt vulnerable, trying to make sense of the maelstrom of emotions churning through her.

She didn't feel any more ready to face him now.

Instead of lying here she should have got up immediately and gone to her room. She needed to process every incredible moment they'd shared.

She'd love to think she'd chosen not to leave because she wasn't a coward.

In fact, she hadn't been sure her legs would support her. Her bones felt like jelly and whole swathes of her body seemed to have turned to mush.

Or maybe that was her brain. Because she'd been thinking ridiculous things about Cesare, as if that shocking combination of tenderness and firmly leashed male power as they made love meant something important and personal.

Annoyance at herself and at him for being so contrary and confounding made her frown. She opened her eyes to see him standing, hands on hips, surveying her across the bed.

Hair tousled, jaw darkening, body…well, frankly superb. He was devastating.

So much for assuming sex would cure her attraction.

A warm weight stirred inside. A sensation she should not be feeling after—could it really be three orgasms?

Heat scored her cheeks and she scrambled up to find the top sheet and drag it over her.

At least her arms worked. She still wasn't sure about her legs.

'I'll go soon.'

'No need. I just wondered if you'd like a bath.' He paused. 'In case you're sore.'

Ida drew a slow breath, trying to read his face. She'd told him she wasn't experienced but hadn't been explicit. Had he been disappointed?

The gentle throb between her legs, courtesy of their enthusiastic coupling, told her not to be stupid. Yet she couldn't help wondering.

'What are you thinking, Ida?'

Great. With her pale skin he'd see the flush rising in her throat and cheeks. It was the bane of her life.

'No, thanks. I don't want a bath.'

Still he seemed to be waiting, the muscles around his shoulders and neck standing taut as if something worried him. Could it be the fact she'd given him her virginity?

'I'm not sore. I'm good. Just far too relaxed to move yet.'

Though she'd have to shift soon. She wasn't naïve

enough to expect Cesare wanted her to share his bed through the night. He'd specified sex only.

'I'm glad you feel okay.'

He wasn't effusive but maybe she'd guessed right, for the rigid set of his shoulders eased as he drew back the sheet and got in beside her.

That surprised her. She'd thought he'd dress again and expect her to as well.

Instantly every nerve ending sparked. In anticipation? But he didn't touch her, instead propping himself on one arm, his gaze on her.

'You're not as I remember you, Ida.'

She rolled onto her side to face him, head on the pillow. He really did have the most comfortable bed.

'You said that before. You make it sound like I've changed.' Which she undoubtedly had. 'But you never really knew me.'

'So I'm beginning to realise.'

She waited. Now he'd pepper her with questions about her grandfather, or the strip club, or her supposed role in the blackmail.

Instead the silence stretched so long she felt herself ease further into the mattress, deep-seated lethargy and a sense of peace filling her despite Cesare's watchful stare. Great sex was exhausting as well as exhilarating, she discovered. On top of that she was still worn out from stress and long hours working.

Eventually Cesare reached out and took her hand, drawing it across the sheet towards him.

'What's the problem with your hands?'

She took a moment to register his words. Then she looked to where her fingers threaded through his olive-toned ones. His fingers were long and there was a drift of dark hair on the back of his hand. In contrast her hand was pale, except for the blotches of pink and areas of peeling skin.

Instinctively Ida made to withdraw her hand, but he held it firmly, his thumb stroking a slow rhythm across her knuckles.

Of course he'd noticed her hands. He'd kissed her all over. She'd just been too busy swooning to think about it.

'A reaction to wearing rubber gloves.'

After years of wearing them for work her skin had suddenly become sensitive.

His gaze turned sharp, and she could almost hear his brain whirring, processing that information.

'Is it painful?'

Ida blinked, surprised, though she didn't know why.

'It can be uncomfortable.'

Itchy. And embarrassing, she now discovered. She mightn't be Cesare's wife in the usual sense but part of her was jealous of those beautiful, glamorous women who flocked around him. She hated feeling inferior, though dermatitis was nothing to be ashamed of. Yet she had nothing to prove to him.

What was wrong with her?

'We'll get some ointment for it tomorrow. Dorotea may have some or we'll buy something.'

She'd run out of medicated cream and hadn't had a chance to get more. 'Thank you.'

It was kind of him.

Or was it that he didn't like looking at her damaged hands? Ida tugged and, when he released his grip, slipped her hand beneath the sheet.

She really should go to her own room.

'That's why you wore the black gloves. To hide your hands.'

Ida kept her tone casual though she didn't like talking about it. 'Dermatitis is bad for business.' She wanted Cesare to remember her as sexy and attractive, not the woman with a skin condition.

'And what business were you in that required rubber gloves?'

For a second she thought he was insinuating some sort of kinky sex game. Except Cesare knew now that she was new to sex.

'I'm a cleaner. I clean houses for rich people during the day and offices at night.' Interesting that Cesare's dark eyes didn't look shocked or pitying. In fact, they simply looked warm and attractive. 'Jo was doing some of my night shifts while I filled in for her at the club.'

Cesare's mouth flattened. Did she imagine it?

Ida suppressed a yawn. She was suddenly incredibly tired. She felt as if she was floating. She blamed this soft mattress, the luxury of a truly comfortable bed and knowing she was safe here from Bruno.

True safety was something she hadn't experienced for a long, long time.

'Tell me, Ida.' Cesare's voice was low and soothing. 'How long have you worked as a cleaner?'

She blinked and tried to focus. Why was he interested? On the other hand, what harm could it do to answer?

'Since I went to London. Four years.' She frowned. 'I'm tired. I should go to my room.'

'If you like. Or you could rest here for a bit first.'

That sounded perfect. Even so, it was puzzling. Surely Cesare wanted the privacy of his room now they'd had sex.

Ida was trying to make sense of that when she slipped softly into sleep.

Cesare lay in the darkness staring at the ceiling.

Ida was snuggled under the covers, her hand tucked under the pillow, like a child.

There was something endearing about the way she'd succumbed suddenly to sleep. One moment they'd been talking. The next her eyelids drooped, and she was out for the count.

Cesare wasn't used to sharing his bed. Strange that he didn't find it disturbing now. But he had a lot on his mind.

He'd expected making love with Ida to be memorable—she'd got under his skin in ways he couldn't explain—yet he hadn't been prepared for their intense passion. For the feelings she engendered in him. And the doubts. She hadn't tried to change his mind about her, yet he was questioning so much.

If Ida had worked the hours she described for any length of time, no wonder she was exhausted.

Why had she been working as a cleaner?

How long had she been hiding from her grandfather?

Cesare had assumed the old man knew where Ida was though he'd claimed not to. He'd probably supported her, laughing up his sleeve as he watched Cesare contend with the far-fetched rumours about his missing wife.

Yet Ida had said she'd worked as a cleaner for four years. It made no sense. She was Calogero's golden charm, his way into the elite society he'd been jealous of all these years. He'd have been delighted with her for marrying Cesare. She had no reason to hide from him.

Cesare needed to get to the bottom of the mystery. Because there *was* a mystery.

Cesare rolled onto his side, watching the woman asleep in his bed.

She was an enigma. Feisty and strong yet vulnerable.

Her virginity had been a total surprise and it altered his view of her.

Lack of sexual experience doesn't mean she was truly an innocent. There was nothing innocent about marrying a man for money and prestige. Or being party to blackmail.

Calogero had made much of his granddaughter's innocence. Maybe that was why she'd still been a virgin, because she knew some men prized that.

The thought stirred nausea.

Yet the woman he'd met yesterday—was it only yesterday?—wasn't the one he remembered.

In London Ida had been angry and abrasive, unimpressed to see him and impatient to end their marriage.

Cesare's thoughts slowed. That had been a blow to his ego. But it didn't explain the compulsion he'd felt, the *need* for her. That predated London.

She'd shown a strength and determination he hadn't noticed before. She'd been open and, as far as he could tell, utterly authentic, both in her dislike of him and later when sharing her body.

Heat beat through his blood at the memory of Ida's soft gasps, that pleased purr and the shocked cries of delight as she'd found her peak. He'd revelled in them all. They'd roused him to a point where pleasure became pain as he tried to keep control.

Cesare had seen Ida's surprise at her own responses and knew the woman in his bed hadn't been playing a game. She'd seemed shocked at her own capacity for pleasure.

Cesare knew he'd finally met the real Ida.

In Rome and before, in her grandfather's home, he'd *felt* her constraint and understood she was careful with her responses to him.

He'd known the woman who'd agreed to marry

him was a façade, a construct made to appear as a sweet, appealing fiancée. There'd been a deep reserve about her and the glances she'd shot her grandfather made it clear she took her lead from Calogero.

In London yesterday Cesare had again sensed constraint, and an unwillingness to let him into her world. She'd built walls around herself.

But in Tuscany something had shifted. Had the walls fallen? Or was Ida allowing him carefully curated glimpses of herself, projecting some new image? Was she playing an even deeper game than before? Having seen women string his father along, he knew about female manipulation.

Cesare sighed. He knew better than to think that because Ida surprised him and he liked what he'd discovered, everything had changed.

He'd never let attraction blur caution or common sense. He'd seen the debacle his father had made of his life, seduced by sex, his judgement flawed, the results disastrous.

He needed the truth about Ida. The more he understood, the greater the possibility of uncovering more ammunition against Calogero. But mainly because this felt like unfinished business between him and Ida.

The sheet had fallen low over her shoulder and Cesare pulled it up, brushing the cool flesh of her back. Instantly she rolled closer.

Cesare stilled, then after a moment's hesitation hauled her to him.

It felt surprisingly good, having her snuggle up. He rarely spent the night with a lover, not wanting to raise expectations of permanency.

This wasn't permanent. Even if, for a while longer, his lover was Ida Brunetti, his wife.

Strange how after years of negative thoughts, the idea of this woman bound with him in marriage didn't spark instant rejection.

It had to be because the end was in sight. Divorce papers signed, Calogero's hold on the company gone and the man himself heading towards a criminal trial, though he didn't know it yet.

As Cesare relaxed, drawing in the alluring scent of sated woman and spring flowers, realisation hit.

Having her here wasn't just good for easing his sexual frustration and digging out information on Calogero. It could provide other opportunities. After the difficulties of the last few years, being seen with his wife, albeit for a short time, could be useful.

Cesare smiled as he tucked her closer.

The compulsion he'd felt to possess Ida hadn't *really* been a compulsion. Of course not.

Cesare didn't let lust drive his actions. He wasn't a slave to emotion. He wasn't weak like his father.

He was being pragmatic. Bedding Ida had been beyond his expectations, but his aim was to excise these intense and disturbing urges. It was safer to sate himself with her now in order to distance himself later. To keep head and heart, or at least libido, separate.

Unlike his father, he'd never allow himself to be a slave to emotion or illusions of love. Because he'd experienced the fallout, seen the damage to family and business. Felt the rejection.

It was a trap Cesare would never fall into.

Ida woke to a delicious sense of peace and comfort. She was warm and cosy and...

Her brain jerked into full wakefulness as she realised her cheek rested on sleek, warm skin and that masculine chest hair tickled her hand.

Cesare.

The man she hated.

Except it wasn't hate she felt.

He'd protected her from Bruno.

And made love to her last night until she saw stars.

Despite knowing it was just sex, it had *felt* like making love. Cesare had been gentle as well as eager, breath-stealingly sensual and potent.

'More.' His deep voice was gruff.

'Sorry?' She hadn't even realised he was awake.

'Do that again. I like it.'

Ida hadn't done anything but inadvertently slide her hand across his chest.

Daylight spilled between the open curtains and, tucked against his shoulder, she had a perfect view of his musculature, of the contrast of dark olive skin against pale, and the hard nub of his erect nipple.

A thrill ran through her. Cesare was aroused.

She drew her hand back across that wide expanse of muscle and felt him tense.

'I want you, Ida.'

She sucked in air, stunned at the impact of that stark admission. Men had wanted her before, but she'd never been tempted. Until Cesare.

This, whatever it was, felt perilous and profound. An elemental force.

Now you're acting like a besotted virgin, confusing sex with something else.

Ida wasn't looking for anything else.

But she did want more of what they'd shared last night. She'd take all the pleasure she could, hoarding it for the future when life would again be a grim struggle for self-sufficiency, trying to keep out of her grandfather's reach.

She leaned down and licked Cesare's nipple then closed her teeth around it, excited by his hissed exclamation and the way his big body rose against her.

An instant later she found herself above him, his hands at her hips, his bare body wonderful against hers.

Ida raised her head and met brown eyes that had turned so dark they seemed black. But there was light in them and a tortured smile on his face that she read easily. She must have looked that way last night.

Last night Cesare had teased her to the edge of bliss time and again, but she felt nowhere near sated. Time was running out. They'd had their night together. If she wanted more, she needed to take it now.

Pushing herself up on hands and knees, she began to move down the bed, pausing to swirl her tongue around his navel and feel a shot of adrenaline as Cesare shuddered and groaned. Then she moved lower, fascinated as his erection swelled before her eyes.

Tentatively she touched him, surprised at the combination of incredible softness over such rigidity. His thighs were rock solid, and his body moved with each stroke of her fingertip. He was so incredibly sensitive.

A smug smile curved Ida's mouth, her hair curtaining her face as she bent over him.

One delicate lick of her tongue and she was blown away. All that virile power, straining for her attention. Another stroke then she settled her lips around him.

Cesare rose, lifting her up and pulling her hair away from her face. Looking up, she met coal-dark eyes and heat punched her, rolling down through her body. When he looked at her like that she felt…

'Come here, Ida. I want you.'

She shook her head. She'd only just begun and had so much to discover.

'I promise you can do that later. But now…' She heard the catch in his voice. 'I need you.'

They were only words. They didn't mean anything. Yet something tumbled over inside because he needed her and admitted it. Besides, as fascinating as this was, she wanted him inside her. The empty clenching between her thighs told its own tale.

Soon she was poised above him, knees wide on the bed while he sheathed himself.

'Guide me in, *cara.*'

Cesare's hands went to her breasts as she gripped him and sank down. Sheet lightning blasted through her. The sensations were like last night. That incredible fullness, the friction. But above all, the way he held her gaze with his sultry, hooded stare as he told her how good this felt.

Ida didn't understand Italian, but she knew they were words of praise and encouragement. His hands worshipped her as his body took up a harder, insistent rhythm and she learned to ride him. It was as if they'd been made for this, for the dancing race that grew faster and more urgent with every buck of his hips and every slide of her body.

Until there it came again. The tendrils of fire, the combustion, the white-hot light that caught her just as Cesare called her name and pulled her, shuddering, onto his chest. He wrapped her in his embrace as the world spun and bliss took her, and she felt the hard pump of his orgasm deep within.

Sharing this with Cesare felt elemental. Too profound for words.

Ida just hoped it wasn't addictive.

CHAPTER ELEVEN

THEY BREAKFASTED IN a secluded arbour. The air was warm and scented and before them tranquil gardens stretched towards a landscape of golds and greens, the undulating hills of Tuscany.

Ida had seen the view yesterday but was still entranced. Shifting shadows and colours painted an ever-changing scene. It was even more beautiful than she'd imagined.

Or maybe that was because her blood still fizzed with elation after last night. It had been a revelation. An interlude of glorious joy that cast her grim, difficult world into the shadows, just for a while.

She wished their night together hadn't ended. One night hadn't quenched her desire. If anything, it had taken her awareness of Cesare, her fascination, to a higher level. Her body hummed just from being so close.

But since leaving his bedroom neither had mentioned the night they'd shared. Ida because it felt momentous and far too new for idle conversation.

And Cesare? She couldn't tell what he felt. He was the perfect, solicitous host, but he didn't touch her.

Ida was surprised at how much she wanted him to.

Cesare leaned towards her. 'Coffee?'

Its rich fragrance hit her nostrils like a benediction. In London her budget was so tight she had only powdered instant.

'Yes, please.' She eyed the basket of pastries warm from the oven. 'This is glorious, thank you.'

'Thank Dorotea. She did all the work.'

That made Ida look at him as he passed her cup.

Cesare had already revealed a considerate side. Yet how many men, especially wealthy men, truly appreciated the work others did for them?

Her view was coloured by her grandfather, who treated staff like automatons rather than people. But interactions with rich clients in London had been the same. They expected her to be invisible as she cleaned. Most saw themselves as innately superior, ever ready to criticise but not praise or appreciate.

But not, it seemed, Cesare.

She thought of how he'd taken time to reassure Jo, who was nervous after her assault. The easy way he'd chatted with staff in the London hotel and on the trip here. He noticed other people. More, he treated them as equals.

Ida liked that.

'I'm lucky to have her,' Cesare added as he passed the basket of baked goods. 'Dorotea takes everything in her stride, is always prepared and is a fantastic cook.'

Ida took a *cornetto*, the Italian version of a croissant, and another pastry. She was starving.

'She's worked for you a long time?'

'Years. Dorotea was my grandfather's house-keeper before I came to live with him as a child.'

'You lived with your grandfather?'

Cesare reached for a pastry. 'He brought me up. I was fortunate to have such a great role model.'

Unlike *her* grandfather, she mused as she bit into light, flaky pastry. Luckily, she hadn't had to live permanently with the old man. The notion made her skin crawl.

'What's wrong?'

She looked up to see Cesare leaning back in his chair, his indolent posture at odds with that alert gaze. But Ida didn't want to talk about her grandfather.

'I was just surprised. I knew you lost your mother when you were very young, but I hadn't realised your father died when you were a child too.' She'd thought he'd died not long before their wedding.

Cesare's expression blanked and she had the feeling she'd crossed some unseen boundary. Then he shrugged and sipped his coffee.

'He didn't. But he wasn't the paternal type. My father had his own interests and found it easier not to have a kid cramping his style. Plus, he did a lot of travelling for business. He didn't stay in one place long.'

Cesare's posture was relaxed but his eyes, and that edge to his voice, indicated his father's rejection had cut deep.

'I'm sorry. That must have been tough.'

A week ago, she'd never have imagined Cesare sharing anything so personal with her. Or her feeling sympathy for the boy he'd been, shuffled off to be cared for by someone else. It was something they had in common, though their circumstances were very different.

She knew what it was to be wrenched from parents and transplanted into an unfamiliar new world.

He shrugged. 'It worked out well. My grandfather raised me here in Tuscany and I couldn't have asked for a better childhood.'

There was no mistaking Cesare's affection for the man who'd raised him. Ida felt another bond of shared experience.

'My childhood was like that too,' she offered. 'Warm and happy. My mother was loving and had a great sense of humour. And Dad was patient, always ready to listen and play. He told great bedtime stories too.'

She paused, surprised at her urge to share such memories with Cesare. But this wasn't the cold man who'd turned on her after their wedding.

She'd discovered hidden depths to Cesare. Not just his sensual, passionate nature, but also a level of respect, warmth and understanding that drew her.

'Ah. My *nonno* wasn't quite like that. He wasn't into playtime or stories. But he was patient. He taught me right from wrong, by example as much as anything. Everything I know about honour, family tradition and responsibilities, I learnt from him.

And about business.' Cesare's mouth twisted. 'For some reason my father didn't inherit his business savvy. That's why the company became vulnerable to Calogero.'

Ida took her time processing that. It sounded as if Cesare's *nonno* was an admirable man, yet she wondered what it would be like, brought up by someone focused on business and responsibility. Surely a child needed warmth and understanding too? The chance simply to be a child?

Was it telling too that Cesare brought the conversation back again so quickly to the family business?

She suspected that, for all his privilege, his childhood hadn't been as carefree and joyous as hers. That he'd had duty and tradition drummed into him. No wonder he'd been ready to do anything, even give in to blackmail, to save the family business built up over generations.

'*You* didn't go to live with your grandfather.'

Cesare's observation dragged her back to the present. 'You know about that?'

He sipped his coffee then lifted his shoulders in a shrug that was intrinsically Italian yet innately his. 'I hired investigators to find you. They researched where you'd lived before, hoping for leads, and discovered you'd spent years in Scotland, rather than with Calogero in London.'

It was a statement, yet she heard the question.

'And you want to know why.'

Ida's voice flattened. It was one thing to share

memories of a happy childhood and a fragile sense of connection. Now she suspected his curiosity was because he wanted to learn more about his enemy, her grandfather, rather than from interest in her personally.

Had she expected a night in Cesare's bed would change things?

Ida swallowed the metallic taste of disappointment.

'Only if you want to tell me, Ida.' Cesare's voice dropped to a low note she'd heard in bed when he'd reined himself in to ensure her pleasure. 'I'm curious about you.'

Ida snapped her gaze up and saw a warmth that contradicted her assumption. Maybe his interest *was* personal.

Something shifted in her chest. Her heart thudded and once more she experienced that phantom sensation from last night. The feeling that together they were on the cusp of something bigger than either of them. Bigger than revenge or family feuds.

Deliberately she looked away, telling herself not to read too much into Cesare's words. They weren't enemies now, but she'd be foolish to think they'd ever share a meaningful relationship as she'd once dreamed.

Her crush on him had dwindled to mere physical attraction.

And if you tell yourself that often enough, you

might actually believe it. The man's haunted you for years, even after that dreadful scene in Rome.

'Forget I mentioned it, Ida. Are you ready for another coffee?'

'No, thanks.'

Instead, she took another bite of buttery pastry and almost sighed her pleasure.

She'd learned to appreciate simple delights when they came her way. It was self-defeating to fret over Cesare's feelings for her. Or lack of them. He'd rescued her from Bruno and her grandfather. He'd given her sanctuary and a night to remember. She should be thanking him.

Besides, sitting in the dappled shade, relaxed over this lovely breakfast, Ida felt an ease and wellbeing she hadn't felt in years.

No, she decided. Last night hadn't been a mistake. It had been a gift.

'I didn't live with my grandfather because he didn't want me,' Ida said finally. 'He doesn't care for anyone but himself. My parents had cut off contact with him. I didn't even know he was alive. When they died my mother's cousin Kate took me in and I moved to her in Scotland.'

Cesare saw her wistful expression and hesitated to probe. But his curiosity was too great. Not so much now about Ida's relationship with her grandfather but about Ida herself. The more he discovered the more intrigued he grew.

Though the way she spoke about Calogero, in that cool, tight voice, made him wonder if she'd truly been the old man's willing protege.

The idea made everything inside him still.

'You were happy with her?'

Ida lifted one shoulder. 'Eventually. It took some adjustment, for all of us.'

Surely that was an understatement. She would have been distressed and grieving, torn from the world she'd known.

By contrast it had been a relief for Cesare when he'd come to live here. He'd thrived in a world of structure and stability, knowing his *nonno* cared for him, even if he wasn't demonstrative.

In a funny way Ida's attempt to downplay how hard that time must have been reminded him of his *nonno*, with his reticence and profound integrity.

Cesare watched Ida's gaze turn to the garden and wondered if she saw another landscape entirely. She looked so self-contained. Yet as a child, it must have been a terrifying experience. He couldn't remember his mother and hadn't been heartbroken by his father's death, yet he remembered the pain when his grandfather died.

'*All* of you? Your mother's cousin had a family?'

The investigator's report hadn't mentioned it. Just that she lived in a small community.

'No. Just me.' She caught his stare and went on. 'Kate ran an artists' commune. There were a few women who lived there permanently and others who'd come for a summer or a few weeks.'

'That must have been…interesting.'

Cesare tried to imagine growing up surrounded by artists on an isolated island.

Ida's mouth tucked up at the corner and he felt it like the caress of fingers down his sternum, heat spreading through his chest. He wanted, as he'd wanted from the moment she'd stepped from the house, to gather her close and lose himself in her sweet body.

It took all his determination to keep his distance, not take her back to bed.

It didn't help that her dress was the colour of crushed raspberries and reminded him of her pretty nipples that peaked so easily, begging for his attention. Or that the narrow straps left her shoulders bare.

'It *was* interesting,' she said with another small shrug. 'Kate had been a teacher and home-schooled me. But I learned a lot more than was on the curriculum.'

'You learned from the other artists?'

She hadn't spoken about being an artist. Surely he'd have remembered if she had? But then, he'd been so focused on Calogero and countering his schemes, how much attention had he really paid to Ida before their marriage?

Enough to want her. That had never been in doubt. He'd carried it like a badge of shame because lusting after his enemy's granddaughter was weakness when he needed to be strong.

Cesare didn't feel that way now. Life, his feelings, and above all Ida were far more complex than he'd once imagined. He leaned in, waiting for her answer.

'I'm a competent potter.' She ticked off one finger then another. 'I can spin, weave and make felt. I'm told my lino cuts show real flair, though I'll never make a painter.'

Her wry amusement was deeply appealing, and Cesare felt his mouth twitch in response.

'Plus I have some talent at making jewellery.'

'Is that what you want to do? Make jewellery?'

Her eyes met his, that soft, delicate green bright and clear. 'No. Those women were real artists. I just picked up skills because I had time and opportunity.'

'And there wasn't much else to do on your island?'

Her eyebrows rose as if he'd revealed the pity he felt for a girl wrenched from her home and stuck in such a place.

'It wasn't that bad. I learned German from Traudl and she told the best stories. She was an illustrator and spun tales about dragons and witches and the most amazing places. Peggy had been an accountant and taught me baking and bookkeeping. Beatrice taught me ballet.' Cesare heard the rising inflection of enthusiasm as Ida paused, leaning down to rub her ankle. Then she caught his gaze on her and straightened. 'Zara taught me self-defence.'

This time her smile was more of a grimace and Cesare wondered if Ida had ever needed to use those defensive techniques. His stomach rolled over.

'It sounds like a well-rounded education. Much more varied than mine.' He paused. 'So how did your grandfather fit into your life?'

Ida's expression shuttered. 'He was legally my guardian, though Kate brought me up. The year I turned twelve, he insisted I start visiting him in London. It didn't matter that he was a stranger or that Kate had reservations. He threatened to take me from her if I didn't obey.'

Cesare swore under his breath. A man who'd threaten to take an orphaned child from a place where she'd found sanctuary was barbaric. But that tallied with all he knew of Calogero.

'Didn't you want to see London and meet your grandfather?'

She met his eyes, moving the crumbs of flaky pastry on her plate. 'I can't help you bring him down, you know. I don't have that sort of inside information. So if you're hoping I'll reveal some juicy nugget about his business or his plans, you'll be disappointed.'

Her words sliced deep, leaving Cesare feeling surprisingly guilty.

He took a moment before replying.

'You're right. That was one of the reasons I wanted you to stay. Any information I can get about him is helpful. But...' He held up his hand as she leaned away from him. 'I'm genuinely curious about you. Not because I'm mining for things to use against the old man.'

'That's what you *would* say.'

Reluctantly he nodded. 'True. But in this case my intentions aren't so devious.' He shook his head, hampered by the long-standing distrust between them. 'It's frustrating that there's nothing I can say that will convince you to believe me.'

To his surprise Ida laughed. A husky chuckle that rippled through him like a beckoning hand. 'Believe me, Cesare, I know the feeling.'

Their eyes met and something blazed between them. He was tempted to label it desire, but it felt like more. Understanding? Regret? Rueful acceptance?

For the first time in his life his subconscious was outpacing logic. His responses to Ida seemed to come from a deeper, mysterious, visceral level, hitherto untapped.

His grandfather had taught him caution, strategic thinking and good planning. Now instinct threatened to take over.

It felt dangerous and unprecedented. Yet too powerful to ignore.

'You're saying I jumped to conclusions about you.'

Ida lifted one shoulder then looked away, biting into her pastry.

Had he done that? Was the past not as he'd imagined?

Had he let his hatred of Calogero taint his view of Ida?

Certainly the things he'd learned about her in the last day and a half gave him pause. She surprised him at every turn.

'I'm willing to believe circumstances weren't as black and white as I thought,' he said, watching her eyes widen. 'I promise to listen to whatever you want to tell me.'

Cesare prided himself on hearing all sides of a dispute before making a decision. The glaring exception had been his assessment of Ida's character. The evidence had pointed to her involvement in Calogero's schemes but had Cesare had *all* the evidence before he judged her?

He wouldn't bully her about it, however much he wanted to know. Once, in the flush of fury at being forced into marriage, he might have. But no longer.

'It's your decision, Ida. If you'd rather not talk about it, I'll respect that.'

CHAPTER TWELVE

HE RESPECTED HER right to privacy?

Ida stared. But those espresso-dark eyes were sincere.

She sat back, stunned.

She'd discovered a new side to Cesare in the past two days. He might be strong and decisive, bossy in fact, but not in a way she couldn't handle. Standing up to Cesare actually brought an illicit tingle of excitement. He wasn't like her grandfather, who met opposition with vicious rage.

Ida knew Cesare wanted to discover everything about her relationship with the old man, hoping for details to help bring him down. Yet instead of bullying her he gave her space.

He put her feelings before his need to know. That was a first in her life.

Ida had told herself she didn't care what Cesare thought of her. Even if he did come to accept she wasn't the woman he'd assumed her, what was the point? She'd leave soon and they'd never see each other again.

But it *did* matter. Mattered far more than she'd imagined.

She wasn't some downtrodden woman who worried about how others saw her. She'd learned to be self-sufficient and her recent struggles had reinforced that.

Yet for some reason, she hated the idea of Cesare believing she was in league with her grandfather. If anything, she and Cesare were allied in their disdain for the man.

She licked a lingering crumb from her bottom lip then finished her coffee.

'Of course I was excited to see London. And I was curious to meet my grandfather. The first time.'

Cesare's eyebrows lifted at the words *first time*, but he said nothing.

'He wasn't anything like I expected.' Ida paused, remembering her nervous excitement as a young girl taken to an ostentatiously large house that felt neither warm nor welcoming. 'He wasn't interested in me as a person or in our doing anything together.'

She'd imagined outings to the zoo or the fabled London stores or even to see the crown jewels.

'What was he interested in?'

'Making sure I could pass muster in polite society.' Ida's mouth twisted. 'Checking I wasn't growing up wild. He wanted a demure, presentable granddaughter who knew what cutlery to use at a fancy dinner. Who could hold her own in polite conversation, no matter what the setting.'

'So he did take you out?'

Ida shook her head. 'He employed someone to do that.'

'A nanny?'

She laughed, but to her ears the sound was bitter.

'Never anything so simple. In the beginning it was someone who taught elocution and deportment. He worried I might acquire a Scottish accent.'

'Would that have been so bad?'

'It wasn't what he wanted.'

Ida remembered her second visit, when she'd deliberately adopted a rich Scottish burr. It hadn't lasted a day. He'd thrashed it out of her.

She reached for her coffee, only to find the cup empty.

'I learned to waltz, as well as how to curtsey in a long dress. As I got older I went with art experts to gallery openings and museums and with a chaperone to gala events so I could learn to mingle and not feel overwhelmed. I went to afternoon tea at fancy hotels and had dinner with strangers.'

'He wanted you comfortable at social events.'

'Not all social events. High-society ones.'

She watched that sink in, a frown creasing Cesare's forehead. She thought of stopping there but the flow of memory was too strong and with it came words, tumbling out.

'After every outing he got a detailed report from his expert on how I'd fitted in. Whether I held my own in conversation. How I stood, my posture, whether I'd used the right cutlery or spoken too loudly. If I'd smiled at the right people. Whether I fitted in.'

'And if you didn't?'

Cesare's expression was serious. As if he already understood. Which he probably did, since he knew her grandfather so well.

'I learned it was better not to disappoint him.'

Strange how cathartic it was to share this. As if in doing so she threw off some of the burdens she'd kept to herself so long.

She never spoke of that time. With Kate she'd kept her comments general, knowing the whole truth would upset the woman who'd taken her in. Later, when she'd understood her grandfather's character and that he wouldn't hesitate to follow through with his threats to keep Ida and to harm her cousin, she'd had even more reason not to share her experiences.

'He hurt you?'

Ida met Cesare's blazing stare and read anger there. Not at her, but at her grandfather.

It was so long since someone had wanted to be her champion. Warmth spread through her, curling tendrils of heat that had nothing to do with attraction or desire. She felt *seen*.

'I'd rather not talk about it.'

Cesare's mouth flattened as if he intended to argue. Then he nodded. More proof that he'd abide by her wishes.

Something inside her chest lifted, light with pleasure.

'We weren't close.' Ida repressed a grimace. 'I'd visit London every year and it was both intensive training and an inspection to see if I lived up to his expectations.'

'Of course you did.' At her surprised stare Cesare continued. 'When we met you seemed almost too perfect. Poised and well groomed. You never seemed to find it difficult to make conversation, but you didn't chatter. Whenever we went out you were comfortable and confident.'

Ida remembered it differently. She *had* been nervous because Cesare was the epitome of her girlish yearnings. She'd wanted him to like her, not simply because her grandfather wished it. Cesare was not only tall, dark and handsome but also gravely courteous and with a delicious Italian accent that curled around her heart and made it sing.

She'd fallen for him, building up a fantasy that he cared for her and would sweep her away to a new life far from her grandfather's influence.

'He was grooming you, wasn't he?'

Ida nodded. 'He wanted me to fit into the sort of society that he never mixed with. Yet he didn't want me in boarding school with a set of privileged girls. He thought I might learn bad ways.' And maybe meet boys. 'It wasn't until after we married that I understood his goal. When you explained it all.'

Cesare stared at her, two vertical lines carved down his forehead. But instead of instantly rejecting her words, he seemed to mull them over.

'I didn't know he was blackmailing you. I believed you when you said it suited you to marry. I thought you wanted a hostess.' Though she should have realised that was wrong. Why choose her when there were so many gorgeous, sophisticated women? 'Plus I leapt at the chance to get away.'

She waited for Cesare to argue. Instead, he seemed to withdraw as if lost in thought.

'My grandfather had become more demanding and restrictive. He even chose the clothes I wore in London. I had to look demure and wear only pale colours because he said they were more *suitable*.'

Suitable for a virgin, though she didn't say that.

He'd threatened dire consequences if she ever tried to date. Because he saw her virginity as an asset to make her attractive to the right bridegroom, his ticket into high society. If the chance to blackmail Cesare hadn't arisen, he'd have pushed her to marry someone else he'd chosen.

'He wasn't your guardian when we met. You were an adult, and he had no legal hold over you. Why were you living with him when I visited?'

'You think he'd let me go just like that? After the years and money he'd invested in me?'

To defy her grandfather would have meant danger for herself and for those she cared about.

'You were scared of him even then?'

A pulse of something throbbed between them. Like a heavy heartbeat, thickening the air. As if once again she and Cesare were linked, not physically like last night, but in shared understanding.

She breathed deep, telling herself to stop imagining things.

'Any sane person would be scared of crossing Fausto Calogero.' She broke eye contact and turned towards the glorious view. It felt wrong to discuss the man who was a sinister, threatening presence in her life in this lovely place. 'Can we change the subject? I don't want to talk about him now.'

She wanted to make the most of her time here. All too soon she'd have to face her troubles. Finding a secure place, starting over, staying hidden.

'Of course.' Cesare paused. 'Thank you for telling me.' Then he was on his feet. 'I'll get us some fresh coffee.'

Ida watched him go, following his loose-limbed stride. He was a man easy in his skin. A great lover. Surprisingly caring. Most amazing of all, he'd heard her out without interrupting. He'd *listened*.

Yet why would he believe her when she'd given no hard evidence to back her claims?

She was grateful he was sensitive enough not to push for details about life with her grandfather. It was a time she'd rather forget. She stretched out her legs, rotating her feet to prove the sudden ache in her right ankle was pure imagination, a reminder of her grandfather's brutality.

What did Cesare think of her now? He'd been surprisingly easy to speak to, not even baulking at her explanation that she'd believed he'd wanted to marry her.

But she hadn't been entirely truthful.

She'd let him believe she'd agreed to the marriage because she didn't dare cross Fausto Calogero.

That was true. She'd seen no way to escape her grandfather's control. But she hadn't wanted to defy him when he'd insisted she marry Cesare. She'd *wanted* the wedding. Wanted the man who was, for just a little longer, her husband.

That was one truth she couldn't reveal.

Cesare carried the tray of fresh coffee from the kitchen, relieved to be doing something.

Sitting at the table, watching Ida's expression as she spoke of how Calogero had planned to use her even from childhood to further his schemes, had been difficult.

He'd wanted to jump up from the table and pace. To curse and berate himself for not considering the possibility that she, too, had been Calogero's victim. That she'd been too scared to defy him.

Cesare stepped out into the sunshine and paused, soaking up the warmth, a counterpoint to the chill in his belly. It had started when Ida spoke of her visits to Calogero but had really taken hold during her silences. When she'd refused to confirm whether Calogero had harmed her. When she'd said no sane person would cross the man.

Given the litany of crimes for which the old man was being investigated, many brutally violent, Cesare knew she'd suffered.

He abhorred the idea of Ida being under his control.

Cesare had no doubt that she told the truth. That haunted look in her eyes had made his skin crawl.

Yet he'd read strength in her composure and a lurking hint of bitter humour that twisted her lips as she skated over things too painful to discuss.

He admired her.

When they'd met, he'd never imagined her to be anything other than his scheming enemy's pampered pet.

Hearing her story had shaken him.

He'd been so committed to his own goals, protecting his extended family and those dependent on the company, he'd not taken time to consider Ida might be an innocent caught up in Calogero's schemes.

Guilt tightened his chest and roiled through his belly. How callous and superior he'd been. How blind!

The coffee cups on the tray Dorotea had provided rattled as he drew in a horrified breath.

All this time he'd prided himself on being decent and honourable. On having purpose and a plan which was finally bearing fruit as the forces of the law inched closer to arresting Calogero.

But for all his lofty ideals, Cesare suddenly saw himself stripped bare.

He was as flawed as his father, the man he'd despised for so long.

He'd let passion, in his case anger rather than lust, blind him to the truth.

It was even worse than that. His father had let his libido and his weakness for pretty women blind him. He'd allowed gold-diggers to pull the wool over his eyes with fake adoration and words of love.

Cesare had only himself to blame. Only Calogero had made him think Ida was privy to the blackmail scheme. If Cesare had been thinking straight, he'd have taken time to question that. Instead, he'd let fury rule him. Fury not just at the outrageous scheme and the threat to those he cared about. But because the old villain had foisted on him a woman who, despite everything, made him want to forget business and revenge and think only of her.

Letting passion rule his thoughts and actions was against everything he'd learned from his *nonno*. A weakness he'd seen in his father and been determined to avoid.

Cesare grimaced. So much for learning from his father's dire example.

He straightened his shoulders and walked on.

Ida was staring into the distance as if lost in the beauty of the landscape. Or remembering her difficult past.

And he'd added to her pain. The things he'd said in Rome... Shame thickened his throat.

As Cesare approached, he saw she'd crossed one foot over her knee, her fingers rubbing her ankle as if in pain. She'd done that before.

'Have you injured yourself?'

Her gaze darted to his as he put down the tray

and took his seat. An instant later she had both feet on the ground.

'Not at all.' She reached for a cup, pausing to inhale the aroma. He guessed it was an excuse not to meet his eyes. 'The coffee here is wonderful. I'll miss it.'

'Then don't go.'

She jumped, spilling coffee on herself. 'Sorry?'

Cesare offered a napkin, but she put the cup down and sucked the hot liquid on her hand.

Something shifted inside him. Not guilt. Desire. He tried to force it away. Surely it was wrong to think about sex with Ida when he'd just discovered how badly he'd treated her.

Weakness for sex had been his father's trademark. Maybe they were more similar than Cesare had thought. This morning was full of disquieting revelations.

'Stay for a while. You're not in a rush to get back, are you?'

Ida surveyed him from under lowered brows. 'But we've had our night together.'

Cesare couldn't help it. Despite the turbulent mix of guilt, regret and shock writhing inside him, he laughed. 'It's going to take more than one night to satisfy either of us, don't you agree?'

He reached over and touched her hand. Instantly awareness stroked through him, lush and warm.

Her eyes met his and he read a matching enthusiasm in those soft green depths. He'd seen that expression last night and earlier this morning when Ida had lost herself to bliss in his arms.

Longing ripped through him.

He wanted her again.

Yet it wasn't just her body he craved. There was something about the way Ida turned to him in the throes of passion. The intriguing combination of strength and vulnerability he'd discovered over the past couple of days. Her proud determination not to be an object of pity.

She deserved better from him.

'I admire you, Ida.'

She looked shocked. 'You do?'

Cesare inclined his head. 'Not many people would have coped with what you've been through. That man dictating your life. The losses you've suffered. Starting over with nothing and no one.'

His skin crawled as he thought about it. He'd contributed to her woes and that shamed him. 'You've faced hardship with grace and dignity.'

She goggled at him as if he'd grown two heads and he couldn't blame her. Not long ago he'd been ready to believe the worst of her.

'You believe me?'

'I do.' Gently he wrapped his fingers around her hand, waiting to see if she'd withdraw. Yet she didn't and he was grateful. 'I acted despicably in Rome. I was so wound up, hating how I'd been manipulated and how powerless I felt, I took out my hatred on you. I never stopped to think that I wasn't the only one he'd forced to do his bidding.'

Cesare's chest rose on a deep sigh as he released her. 'I'm sorry, Ida. If I hadn't been so proud and caught up in my own problems, I wouldn't have treated you that way. You wouldn't have had to run off into the night.'

Pain scraped his throat as he swallowed.

'Thank you.'

He couldn't read her expression. Couldn't tell how she felt about his apology. But she'd accepted it. That was a beginning.

Cesare knew it would take a long time before he felt he'd made it up to her. If he could ever find a way.

'No, thank you for telling me the truth. I realise they're not happy memories.'

Ida shrugged and once more he felt that tug of admiration that she should be so strong after she'd been through so much. Perhaps *because* she'd been through it.

'And I need to be clear.' He held her gaze. 'I'd like you to stay, partly because I want to make up for the mistakes I made before and the way I judged you. I'll also do everything necessary to protect you from Calogero. You'll be safe from him.'

That got a response. A quick blink of stunning green eyes that looked suddenly overbright.

'Thank—'

'Don't thank me! It's the least I can do.' He

paused. 'I want to continue what we started last night, for as long as it suits us both. But the invitation to stay and my protection aren't conditional on sex.'

'You said before that you'd wait for me to come to you.'

How arrogant he'd been.

'Stay and have a vacation. With luck it won't be too long before Calogero faces justice for his crimes.'

'Really?' She looked stunned as if she thought her grandfather untouchable. Not surprising given the way he'd controlled her life for so long.

'So I'm told.' If all went to plan, he'd spend the rest of his life behind bars, but Cesare didn't say that. Calogero was cunning and would put up a fight.

'I could show you a little of Tuscany.' The revelation of her past made him want to give her something special. It wasn't much but sharing some of his favourite places might go some way towards lessening his guilt over what had gone before. 'Do you want to see Florence, Siena, San Gimignano?'

'But it will complicate things if we're seen together. We're getting a divorce. If you're seen with me now…' Her voice sharpened. 'Or is that the idea? To prove I'm alive and well and you didn't dispose of me?'

Right now, that was the last thing on his mind. The fact Ida had instantly thought of it proved she'd seen too much of how her grandfather's devious mind worked.

And that she didn't fully trust Cesare.

Who could blame her? He had a long way to go to prove himself to her.

Why did it feel vital to do just that?

'I ignore gossip about our marriage.' It had been the only way to cope with so many outrageous stories circulating. At first, they'd wounded his pride, until he decided to focus on saving his business. That left no time for anything else. 'I live my life to suit myself.' He paused to let that sink in. 'I want you to stay. But I see no reason to shut ourselves away here. We have nothing to hide.'

Still, she looked doubtful. Cesare needed another argument because he wasn't ready for Ida to leave.

'Think of it as a holiday. An opportunity to relax and have fun.' She'd had precious little fun.

Ida wavered. He saw it in her eyes.

'And imagine how annoyed your grandfather will be if he discovers you're here with me where he can't get to you. Wouldn't you like, for once, to thumb your nose at the old devil? To do something you want to do, not because you're forced into it?'

Pleasure shot through him at Ida's slow-dawning smile.

And something else, something he preferred not to dwell on. Relief.

CHAPTER THIRTEEN

IDA LEANED BACK in the passenger seat of the open convertible, feeling it cradle her body like an embrace.

As they left the picturesque Tuscan hill town, pealing bells rang out over the low roar of the engine. Late-afternoon sun warmed her shoulders, left bare by her bright summer dress. She snuggled into the deep leather seat and stretched her legs, a pleasant tiredness filling her. She smiled as she flexed her feet. They ached gently from so much walking over quaint cobblestoned streets.

Ida turned to the man beside her and her heart gave a little lurch.

Not simply because he was so charismatic, with his strong features, casual elegance and emphatic air of masculinity. Even the competent way he handled the powerful car was attractive.

Or because last night he'd again taken her to heaven with his lovemaking. Though perhaps that was a tiny part of it.

She felt this profound sense of wellbeing because he'd given her such an incredible, unexpected gift. This glorious day.

She glowed from the joy of it.

'Thank you for today, Cesare. I've enjoyed every minute.'

He turned, dark glasses hiding his eyes, his mouth curving in the tiniest hint of a smile as he turned back at the road. 'I'm glad you liked your first taste of Tuscany.' He paused. 'I'm glad you decided to stay.'

So was she. Incredibly glad.

It was two days since she'd made that decision, yet it felt like a lifetime. As if her old life were a barely remembered nightmare.

That couldn't last. This was a temporary reprieve from Ida's real world. But at least when she returned, she'd have wonderful memories. So wonderful she felt impelled to make him understand.

'I *loved* it. I've never had a day like it.'

'I told you Tuscany is special.'

He didn't understand. He thought she was simply talking about the stunning buildings and pretty vistas. The meandering streets. The cornucopia of produce displayed at the food market.

Ida shook her head. 'The place is lovely, but I meant more than that. It's been a revelation. Not just the architecture and the people. Or even the food.'

She'd adored the food. The lemon *gelato* had tingled on her tongue like a frozen taste of summer. The red wine they'd sampled at a small vineyard had been so rich and full. Their lunch, simple but delicious.

'You've given me…' She searched for the right words, to her chagrin feeling her throat tighten. She didn't *do* emotional.

'Ida? What is it?'

He reached out, his hand squeezing hers.

She felt that immediate rush of pleasure. Was it possible that in just two days she'd become addicted to his touch? It almost felt like Cesare had the power to convince her he could make everything okay.

But life wasn't so simple.

They approached a tight curve in the road and Cesare put his hand back on the steering wheel. Ida told herself she was glad. She felt too much emotion bubbling inside without Cesare's touch befuddling her.

Deliberately she focused on the shadows of dark ochre and plum lengthening across the undulating countryside as the sun dropped.

'It's hard to explain.'

She hesitated, torn between needing to let him know how much today meant and caution at revealing too much.

'Try me. I want to know. I want to understand.'

Ida had spent her life learning to hold in strong feelings, not to share them. Kate was a generation older. She'd cared for Ida and tried her best, but had never been a true confidante, and Ida's grandfather had been the very reason she'd learned to keep her emotions buttoned down.

'Everywhere we went, everything we did, was fun and fascinating. But it's not that. It's the fact you thought about what might appeal and then organised a day that was totally for *me*.'

She heard the tell-tale wobble in her voice and paused.

'Thank you, Cesare. I'll remember today always. It was a lovely gift.'

He'd made her feel special, though she understood his motivations weren't solely about pleasing her.

For the longest time he didn't say anything. Eventually she turned and found him frowning at the road as they swooped down a hill.

Finally, he spoke. The rush of wind past the car must have affected her hearing because he sounded different, his voice hoarse.

'You've never had that before? A time just for you?'

'Not since my parents died.' She stopped. The contrast between her happy childhood and later years was too stark. Even with Kate, Ida had always been conscious that she was an unasked-for burden, though her cousin had never said so. 'Anyway, I want you to know I appreciate it. You've been very generous with your time.'

They could have stayed on Cesare's estate, and she'd have been happy. She adored sex with this man. His tenderness and his urgency, his patient seduction and his outrageously exciting demands. When they weren't making love, she had the run of his pool, his library, the pretty gardens, the cinema room and—

'Usually when women speak about generosity,

they mean dates somewhere expensive or extravagant gifts.'

'You mix with the wrong sort of women.' She shot him a challenging stare and saw his tight smile.

'What about tomorrow?'

'Tomorrow? What about it?'

'Don't you want to go out again?'

Ida frowned. 'It's Monday. I thought you'd be working.' He'd already taken time away from his precious company to track her down in Britain. She hadn't wanted to assume he'd take more time out of his schedule.

'I'm delegating. I keep an eye on the business, but I have very good managers now for day-to-day matters. I thought we might go into Florence.'

Her heart leapt. It was somewhere she'd wanted to see for so long. Ever since those forced art-appreciation lessons in London that had unexpectedly turned into a delight, except for the looming threat of her grandfather's displeasure if she didn't learn well enough.

'I'd like that.'

'Excellent.'

Cesare's nod was curt and his smile absent.

Because for him this isn't about pleasure.

She'd forgotten that. She'd let herself be swept away by emotion.

He wants to take you into the city so you'll be seen together. So word will get back to Fausto.

Because Cesare wants to rub his nose in the fact you're together but not on the old man's terms.

Ida rubbed her hands up her bare arms, feeling chilled despite the sun's warmth.

Or was it more than that? Despite Cesare's dismissive words about not listening to gossip, he'd enjoy showing the world that his missing wife was alive and well and spending her days with him.

Of course that was it. Or at least part of his reason for giving up his time to show her around.

Not because she was special. Because there were benefits.

Ida blinked and stared blindly ahead.

What did you expect? You went into this with your eyes open. You don't expect any man to put you first for your sake alone.

For the first time since he'd taken her to his bed, Cesare felt uncomfortable. Deeply uncomfortable.

What Ida had just told him seemed to strip a layer off his skin.

He flattened his mouth and tried to focus on the narrow road. Yet every thought was on the woman beside him.

Ida would hate to think he saw her as a victim. Yet what she'd said pierced deep. Her words hadn't been a bid for sympathy. He'd heard the ache in her voice, her sincerity, and it had dragged him down to earth with an almighty thump.

He'd thought to give her a pleasant day out. He

was proud of his home region and wanted her to like it too. But any thought of it as merely a fun outing with his temporary lover had shattered.

It humbled him that something so simple meant so much to her.

Against Ida's past his own troubles had been minuscule. Her gratitude made Cesare aware of all the good things he'd had. A stable home. The love of his *nonno* and extended family even though his father had been a disaster as a parent. Wealth and privilege, access to the best educational opportunities and so much that he'd taken for granted.

Safety.

His *nonno* had been a strict disciplinarian but Cesare had never been in physical danger from him. Unlike Ida, whose fear of Calogero had to stem from his capacity for vicious reprisals.

Cesare's skin chilled at the thought of what Calogero would do if he got his hands on her.

'Here we are.' It was a relief to swing off the road, pausing while the electronic gates opened.

Cesare didn't turn to meet her eyes as he would have earlier today when he'd enjoyed watching her delight in each new experience. And basked in her rare, devastating smiles. At first he'd seen them only in bed, but today, increasingly, he'd watched the curve of her lips and felt entranced.

He hadn't realised how jaded and self-focused he'd been until confronted with her innocent joy.

His breath rushed out and his skin prickled with

shame and regret. And deep inside, his determination to bring down her viper of a grandfather glowed white-hot.

They were silent as they entered the villa. Until Dorotea approached with news that there'd been a delivery for Ida.

Cesare followed her into the library. If Calogero had sent some threat…

But Ida smiled as she saw a shabby backpack and a battered cardboard box on the antique desk.

'It's from Jo! But how?'

Already she was opening the backpack. Cesare saw a pair of sneakers and some clothes.

He paused behind her. 'You wanted your parcel delivered to her. My courier returned with your things.'

Even having seen the sparse poverty of that tiny flat, Cesare was stunned by how little Ida owned. He glanced around the room but there was no more luggage.

'Thank you. I never expected you to do that.' Their gazes held and his heartbeat grew ponderous.

'It was nothing.'

She surveyed him for a long time before opening the box and lifting out some books. She ran her fingers over them as if reacquainting herself with old friends. Cesare moved closer, intrigued to know what books Ida treasured when she owned so little.

He saw a cheap photo album and a couple of large folders labelled *Designs*. No fiction titles but a hardcover on art and another on interior design, both battered.

Ida had pulled out her phone and was tapping in a message, presumably to her friend in London.

Cesare, ignoring the fact he had no right to pry, opened one of the folders, discovering neatly handwritten notes, a world of colour and texture, fabrics and furniture design, architecture and—

'Jo says you had someone guard her. Not just at the flat but when she went out.'

Ida looked up from her phone, her expression stunned.

Cesare spread his hands. 'It seemed sensible. Calogero's man could have gone back there to find out more about your plans.' Though he was convinced the old devil now knew precisely where Ida was. 'I didn't want him threatening or hurting her.'

Slowly Ida inclined her head. 'Thank you. I appreciate it.' Her expression remained puzzled.

Had she imagined he'd ignore the danger Calogero presented? Cesare knew the harm he could do. People had died in that factory fire. Others had lost jobs when Brunetti Enterprises hit tough times due to his interference.

Maybe Ida thought Cesare didn't care about anything but getting his revenge on the old man.

That would make him no better than his enemy.

'You haven't mentioned going back to stay with your cousin,' he said, needing suddenly to change the subject.

'That's impossible. Even if I wanted to spend the rest of my life in a remote artists' colony. You worried that Jo might be in danger. The same applies to Kate and her friends. I won't do that to them.'

Ida wasn't the way he'd once imagined her. Neither a gold-digger nor a vamp. Vulnerable yes, and she'd suffered, but she wasn't simply a victim. She was sweet and strong and no pushover.

It was incredible that he'd ever believed she'd tried to claw her way into the aristocracy using his name. Ida was loyal and moved by simple pleasures.

Cesare was drawn by the wonder in her eyes when they made love and when she'd thanked him for their day out. And by her spine of steel.

'What do you want from life, Ida?' Suddenly it was imperative to know. 'What are your plans?'

'Once I'm free of him, you mean?'

There it was again, proof that she lived in the shadow of her grandfather. Not for much longer. Cesare would see her free of him, he swore it.

She didn't answer immediately. Had she lived in hiding so long she hadn't let herself make plans? 'What did you want to be when you were growing up?'

'A dancer. How about you?'

'A fireman,' he replied instantly. 'Funny, I'd forgotten that until now.'

'Let me guess. You wanted to save people?'

'Possibly. But I think it was the lure of driving a big red truck with a loud siren and climbing ladders.'

She laughed and he felt it like ripples under his skin.

'But you didn't have access to a professional dance teacher on your island.'

The sparkle in her eyes dimmed. 'Actually Beatrice, who taught me, had been a prima ballerina. I dreamed of dancing professionally, but I injured my ankle badly.' Abruptly she turned away to repack the books. 'Besides, my grandfather had other plans.'

'I'm sorry.'

She shrugged. 'It doesn't matter. I probably wouldn't have been good enough.'

Perhaps not but Cesare didn't like that she hadn't had a chance to try. 'And now? Interior design?'

Her head lifted sharply then she reached for the folders of what he'd realised were projects.

'Have you worked as a designer?'

She shook her head, her bright hair swishing around her shoulders as she held the folders close. 'As if. I've done a basic online course. That's all. It's hard to get qualifications when you're working all hours to support yourself.'

Ida plonked the folders back into the box, then added the books. Last was the worn photo album. Did it contain pictures of her with her parents?

Compassion filled him for all she'd lost. The opportunities she'd never had. Yet she wasn't after sympathy.

She had to be one of the strongest people he knew.

'How about you, Cesare? If you didn't have your family company, what would you want to be now?'

He leaned his hip against the desk, folding his arms, telling himself not to push her further.

'I have no idea. Since I was a boy I knew I'd work in the family firm. It never occurred to me to do anything else.'

Her eyebrows lifted. 'Really? You had no other driving ambition?'

Perhaps it was that hint of disbelief. Or the feeling he'd short-changed her by not giving an answer when she'd already shared so much. He hated that through most of their dealings she'd had so little agency. Except when they shared their bodies. *Then* there was no power imbalance.

Cesare found himself saying gruffly. 'My one real ambition was *not* to be like my father.'

It was something he'd never admitted, though he was sure his *nonno* had guessed.

Surprisingly he felt no qualms revealing it. The past was the past. Even if his feelings for his *papá* were something he didn't discuss.

Her steady green gaze held his. He saw neither surprise nor judgement there. 'He wasn't a good man?'

Cesare opened his mouth then shut it, forced by her direct question to consider objectively.

'He wasn't a bad man.'

In his younger days Cesare had thought him so. Because he'd been wounded by his *papá's* neglect and lack of interest. Later hurt had morphed into annoyance at how his father's actions had played into their enemy's hands.

'He was weak and selfish. He didn't care about anyone but himself.'

Warmth brushed Cesare's hand and he looked down, surprised to see Ida's fingers sliding across his. Instinctively he captured them.

Her hand fitted his. He noted her chapped skin looked a little better now she'd used the salve Dorotea had provided.

Cesare swallowed. Ida's touch and her silent sympathy felt like a salve on those old wounds that, he now realised, had never healed.

'He hurt you.'

Cesare looked up and read Ida's sympathy. He shook his head. 'I had a wonderful grandfather who loved me. I didn't need my father.'

Ida stepped close, her tantalising scent, like the promise of spring, filtering into his senses. 'Every child deserves the love of its mother and father.'

It hit him then that, while Ida had been orphaned early and struggled since under Calogero's brutality, at least she'd known what it was to have two loving parents. It was there in her quiet confidence, and the concern in those bright eyes.

'He wasn't a brute. He didn't abuse me. He just wasn't interested. He was focused on the woman who was the great love of his life. When she betrayed him or proved herself interested only in money, he'd move on to the next and the next. He had appalling judgement and no time for a child.'

'Maybe he was grieving for your mother.'

Cesare lifted his shoulders. 'Maybe.'

'But that doesn't excuse what he did to you.'

Looking into her grave face, Cesare felt warmth spread through him. Not the potent heat of desire but something steady and comfortable.

Again he shrugged. 'I was okay. I had my grandfather.' Cesare *had* been all right. He'd belonged and been cared for. 'But over time my father grew more unreliable. His work suffered and through it the business. His bad decisions weakened the company, leaving it wide open for Calogero to do his worst.'

Ida frowned.

'What?'

'I know how important Brunetti Enterprises is. Your grandfather drummed that into you, along with your duties and responsibilities. But it's a business. It's not *always* the most important thing. Admitting to pain isn't weakness.'

Ida didn't fully understand. He had a duty not just to his family but also to the thousands whose livelihoods depended on the company. Yet her words trickled through him, an unexpected truth that he couldn't ignore.

He'd think about it later when he was alone. Because he suddenly felt vulnerable as he hadn't been since boyhood, when he'd brimmed with pain and desolation.

Cesare straightened and took her other hand. He dropped his voice to a suggestive rumble. 'If I'm hurt, will you make me feel better?'

Frustration pinched Ida's face. But when he ran his thumbs slowly across her palms then up her bare arms, she shivered voluptuously.

'You're changing the subject.'

Cesare nuzzled her neck, inhaling sweetness. Now he wasn't thinking of diversions but of a need that was raw and real, the more so for the way she'd dug into his emotions and tried to make them better. As if *he* were the one who needed help.

Instead of annoying him, her sincerity moved him. Not that he'd admit it.

'I have a sudden urge to be close to you,' he murmured. 'For comfort.'

It wasn't a convenient ruse or a teasing invitation. It was, he discovered, the surprising truth.

He wanted the comfort of being with Ida. He needed the intimacy of her body joining with his, her kisses drugging his senses and obliterating the shards of old pain.

He lifted his head and met her quizzical stare. 'Please, Ida.'

What she saw in his face he had no idea. But her expression softened as she planted her palm against his cheek.

'Let's go upstairs,' she whispered.

CHAPTER FOURTEEN

CESARE LISTENED TO his cousin enthuse about the new designer he wanted to bring into the haute couture arm of the company. But his thoughts were metres away with Ida.

She looked stunning. Her full-length halter-neck dress of rich crimson clung, gleaming, to her body. Her hair was up in a seemingly casual twist low at the back of her head, and he couldn't take his eyes off her. Even here, among the glitterati at this exclusive charity event, she stood out.

The elite of Europe was attending this prestigious charity event in the Boboli Gardens beside Florence's Palazzo Pitti, quaffing vintage wine and showing off their finery. None held a candle to Ida.

Six weeks she'd been back in his world and still she stole his breath. When he'd suggested she stay on he'd been thinking in terms of days. Weeks had turned into more than a month, yet he wasn't ready for her to go. And not just because Calogero was still at large.

What did it mean that living with her felt like all the best times of his life rolled into one? Did his years of celibacy and tunnel-visioned focus on work skew his perception? Or was it something else?

'Cesare. Did you hear what I said?'

'Sorry, Francesco. My mind wandered.'

Strange. In the past his mind had been like a steel trap whenever business was discussed.

His cousin laughed. 'I can't blame you. Not with your wife looking so charming.'

'She is, isn't she?'

His wife. Funny how the word didn't disturb Cesare as it had in the days when he couldn't wait to be free of her.

Technically she was his wife *for now*. But for the first time in his life, he was living in the moment. Content to take pleasure in Ida without worrying about the future.

The company was doing well. The management team was focused and energised by new opportunities, and he could step back a little. Calogero hadn't raised his ugly head, though Cesare knew he'd be seething at the fact Ida and Cesare were together while there was no benefit to him. Soon, with luck, the various police investigations into Calogero's crimes would bring results.

When they did would Ida leave straight away?

Cesare gripped his glass tighter, his palm suddenly clammy.

'I'm glad the marriage worked out after all,' Francesco said in a low voice.

Cesare nodded but said nothing. What would he say? That it was only temporary? That what they shared was more like a steamy affair than a marriage? That the divorce papers were already signed?

He drained his glass, vaguely noticing the wine wasn't as smooth as he'd thought.

Ida would return to the UK when it was safe.

Cesare would, in some distant future, find a wife who'd help him carry on the Brunetti line. It would be a sensible, convenient marriage.

Too often he'd seen his father chase the fleeting mirage of romance, confusing lust with love. Seen how it turned him into a fool. Cesare had no intention of following in his footsteps.

Ida laughed at something her companion said, the sound as light as the bubbles in her glass. Her head tipped back, drawing Cesare's gaze from her slender throat to her soft lips and that stunning red-gold hair. She had the colouring of a renaissance angel, but Ida was far more vibrant and alluring.

She held her own in this crowd, as she had at every event they attended. Cesare actually relished attending them with Ida beside him. Instead of networking, Cesare had relaxed and enjoyed the company and the art, since it was mainly performance and other art-related events they chose to attend.

He'd had to smother laughter when some of the worst gossips quizzed Ida about where she'd been since the wedding. She'd dealt with them firmly and with apparent ease, making it clear she didn't fear anything they or the press might say about her. That had garnered respect and, while some regarded her doubtfully, she'd generally been welcomed.

Not that it seemed to matter to Ida. Knowing how

she'd struggled these past years and how much of an outsider she must feel, Cesare felt his admiration soar.

He'd been pleased to see signs of a genuine connection between Ida and some of his friends. Like the woman beside her, a talented designer.

The other woman moved away, and Ida turned. Their eyes met with a palpable crackle of connection. Cesare held out his hand to her.

His cousin groaned theatrically. 'Now I've got no hope of keeping your attention.'

Cesare turned to him. 'Serves you right for spending the evening talking business.'

Francesco goggled and Cesare felt almost sorry for him. Once Cesare would have been only too happy to discuss commercial plans at any time. He'd used to attend social events primarily to promote Brunetti Enterprises.

'I'll come to the office tomorrow. You can tell me about it over coffee.'

'I'll look forward to it.' Francesco leaned down to kiss Ida's cheeks as she joined them. 'I don't know what you've done to my starchy cousin, Ida, but he's a changed man. I like it.' He winked and whispered something in her ear before nodding to Cesare and strolling away.

Ida's laughing green eyes surveyed Cesare as he drew her close and draped his arm possessively around her. That felt better. The taut feeling in his chest eased as she nestled closer.

'I like this,' she murmured huskily.

'Good.' His hand slid over her hip and heat built low in his body. 'But it's not enough.'

He didn't give a damn that they were being observed. He wanted her. He wanted a lot more than he could do in this public place. Nevertheless, he found his gaze turning towards the darker corners of the manicured gardens.

Ida slanted him a look that stoked the glowing heat in his belly. 'Maybe we should leave soon. Though Francesco will guess why.'

'Cheeky pup. What did he whisper to you?'

Cesare's voice growled across Ida's sensitive flesh, making her nipples peak. Just as well few guests were clustered in among the lights in this part of the garden.

'Nothing important,' she murmured. 'You know he can't resist teasing.'

I'm glad you're back with him, Ida. You're good for him.

That was what Francesco had said, and heaven help her, but the words had struck home.

Because that was how she felt. That Cesare was good for *her*.

She'd blossomed. Not just sexually, though that was a major and wonderful part of what they shared. Ida felt more comfortable in herself, less at odds with the world. At first, she'd thought it was because she wasn't focused on scraping a living or in fear of being found and punished by her grandfather.

But it was more than that.

In Tuscany, with Cesare, she'd begun to feel whole in a way she couldn't remember feeling, except as a child when the world had been simple and happy.

When she'd felt cared for and valued.

Her time with the man who'd all but kidnapped her in London, the man she'd once hoped never to see again, had grown into something unexpected. Something that excited and terrified her in equal measure.

She didn't want to think about it. Whatever this was, however magical it felt, it wouldn't last.

It wouldn't do to get attached.

'We can't leave yet. I'm giving a speech.' Impatience radiated from him as he shot a look at his watch. 'But I'll keep it short, then we can go home.'

Cesare didn't try to conceal the hungry glint in his eyes as his mouth curled into a slow grin.

Home with Cesare. It sounded perfect.

Except it's not your home, is it? You're living in a fool's paradise, letting a couple of days turn into a fortnight. A fortnight into a month. It's six weeks since you arrived, and you've done nothing concrete about moving on.

Because she didn't *want* to move on.

'Ida? What is it?'

Damn the man for being so acutely observant. Sometimes it felt as if he read her as easily as a book.

Ida searched for a distraction, something to break the spell of Francesco's words and Cesare's magnetism. She looked around, noting there was no one within earshot.

'Will you marry again, Cesare? When this is over?'

His head jerked back, and long fingers dug into her hip. 'Marry?'

'I don't mean straight away.'

Looking into his dark eyes, Ida wished she hadn't asked. Because she'd seen a flash of something unsettling there.

Guilt.

Could it be that Cesare was already planning marriage while having a fling with his soon-to-be ex? She swallowed hard, almost choking on a knot of burning emotion.

But why shouldn't he? This was temporary. Already judicial wheels were grinding their ill-fated marriage into divorce.

Ida made to step away, but he stopped her, his encircling arm like warm steel.

'Why do you ask, Ida? Do *you* have marriage plans?'

Cesare bent so his face was just above hers, his eyes now unreadable. She sensed something new in him, something that reminded her of his fury when they'd met in London.

'Absolutely not!' She paused and hiked her chin higher, ignoring the way it brought her closer to him. 'I don't need a man in my life to make me happy.'

Liar. He makes you happy.

Ida saw Cesare's head jerk back, his jaw flex hard, as if he repudiated her words. But that would imply she'd hurt him.

She digested the idea. Then rejected it. Cesare had made it clear this affair would last only as long as the sparking attraction between them. Which, he'd reiterated, would be transient. Given his greater experience, she had to believe him.

Besides, Ida was no fool. She'd heard Cesare's pain and contempt as he spoke of his unreliable father, consumed by his passion for one beautiful woman after another.

Or had it been a quest for love after the loss of his wife? How much of Cesare's view was shaped by the attitude of the grandfather he'd hero-worshipped?

Not that it mattered. The result was the same. Cesare wasn't a romantic. When he married again, he'd choose someone with a similar background to himself, a suitable CEO's wife. Not a woman like her.

'I can't blame you.' Cesare's words were even, belying the glitter in his eyes. 'The men in your life haven't treated you well.'

Ida put her hand on his arm, feeling the biceps taut beneath the perfect tailoring. 'You've already apologised, Cesare. It's in the past. Let it go.'

She knew he blamed himself for the years she'd

struggled since their wedding. But they'd made her stronger and shown her she'd survive the unknown future that seemed so daunting.

A future without Cesare.

Ida's emotions seesawed wildly. She dropped her hand and spun away. 'It's time we joined the others.'

But Cesare's encircling arm held her close. 'Are you trying to tell me you've changed your mind? You've had enough, Ida? Enough of me?'

His gruff words caught the breath in her lungs and a band of heat squeezed her ribs. Without thinking she shook her head. 'No!'

Ida wasn't ready to leave him. Not yet. Her yearning for Cesare was so potent she tasted the plea forming on her tongue, should he try to send her away.

'Excellent. Because I'm not ready for you to go.'

Cesare smiled that slow, devastating smile that turned her legs to overcooked spaghetti. Relief hit like a blast of summer heat, leaving her weak and trembling. Every nerve ending sparked as he raised his hand to her hair, massaging slowly as he drew her closer.

His eyes looked inky black and sinfully inviting and her heartbeat took up a thunderous rhythm. Instinctively she understood she would always respond to that look. Always feel the heady rush of excitement and affection.

But he didn't kiss her. She didn't expect him to. They never kissed in public.

Because every time their lips touched need rose in crescendo, inevitably leading to far greater intimacies. To their being sated and gasping as they shuddered against each other, hands clutching and breaths mingling.

His hold gentled as he brushed his lips across her temple. 'Hold that thought, *tesoro*.'

Then he led her down to the part of the garden crowded with glittering guests. Ida pressed against him, revelling in the feel of his lean body, powerful and reassuring. Reassuring because, far from wanting to leave him, she couldn't imagine being without him.

Are you really so in thrall to this man?

When had her happiness become linked with Cesare?

The alarm ringing in Ida's head drowned out the noise of the party.

Someone bustled over, asking Cesare to follow. Cesare squeezed her hand, assured her he wouldn't be long, and turned away, leaving Ida with her dazed thoughts.

When had the prospect of parting assumed such dreadful proportions?

Ida knew she'd survive without him. But she didn't want merely to survive. Not any more. The time they'd spent together had taught her that she wanted so much more. She wanted happiness. Companionship. Caring. Waking each day to anticipation and delight. Ending each day in Cesare's arms.

Her heart gave a mighty thump that sent shock waves through her.

When had she fallen for her husband? When he'd spirited her to safety, away from her grandfather? When he'd made gentle, passionate, blazingly beautiful love to her? When he'd listened to her story, even putting together the pieces she'd preferred not to describe in detail?

Maybe when he'd apologised for his past behaviour. Or when she'd discovered he'd taken steps to protect her friend Jo. Definitely when he'd organised for her to visit the interior-design offices of the vast Brunetti portfolio, arranging for her to spend a day there so she could ask questions and see the sort of work they did. When he'd talked about her pursuing her interest in design as if that were the most natural thing in the world. And when he'd begun introducing her to his friends.

Contrary to what she'd expected, Cesare hadn't hidden her away. Nor had he deliberately flaunted her publicly, as if needing to prove something to the scandalmongers who'd thrived on the news of her disappearance.

He'd treated her with respect, thoughtfulness and passion.

She loved it.

She might never feel totally at ease in Cesare's rarefied world, but she'd met enough of his friends to value them as sincere and caring. Which said a lot about the man himself. He was far from the monster she'd once thought him.

'There you are, cousin.' It was Francesco, his smile wide. 'I've brought some people to meet you. Can't have you standing alone while the great man speaks.'

He winked and Ida felt something roll over in her chest. Because of his kindness. Because in the distance she saw Cesare nod approvingly, making her wonder if he'd instigated this.

Because for the first time in forever Ida felt as if she really *was* with family.

Her throat tightened, her nostrils and the backs of her eyes prickling. It was an illusion, of course. She didn't belong here. These people weren't her family.

It was just that here, in Cesare's territory, with him and those around him doing so much to make her welcome, Ida's emotions were strangely wobbly.

After her hellish experiences with her grandfather, this acceptance, this kindness, made her feel too much.

So when, just fifteen minutes later, Cesare forged his way through the applauding throng and held out his arm, she stepped close and looped hers through it. Instantly she felt better, as his warmth and lemony cedar scent enveloped her.

'You're sure you're happy to leave?' he murmured.

Ida pressed nearer, surveying him from under

veiling lashes, hoping he read only invitation in her eyes.

He was so handsome, so dear, that it almost undid her just to look at him. Ida realised she was storing up memories against the time when they parted.

When the time came it would be almost impossible to leave Cesare and return to her real life far away. In the meantime, it *was* impossible to give up this fragile joy until she absolutely had to. 'Yes, please. I want to be alone with you.'

Cesare stiffened and she saw a pulse throb at his temple. 'Whatever you wish, *tesoro.*'

Then they were sweeping through the gardens, past the crowds, almost oblivious to the faces turned their way, the greetings and invitations to pause. Cesare's pace didn't falter, though he scattered greetings and a few promises to meet up another time, before shepherding her outside, past the clamouring paparazzi and into the car that miraculously appeared before them.

Minutes later they were driving through Florence. Even now its beauty brought a lump to Ida's throat. Would she ever return here, or would it be out of bounds for ever because the city reminded her of Cesare?

Ida was so lost in thought she was surprised to realise the car had stopped and someone had opened the passenger door. 'Cesare?'

But he was climbing out. Ida turned towards her open door and saw they were in front of an elegant hotel, her door held open by a smiling staff member. Then Cesare was there, holding out her hand and drawing her towards the gleaming entrance.

'Why are we here?'

His lips brushed her ear as he drew her inside. She shivered as a ribbon of heat uncoiled within her. 'The villa is too far away. I want you *now*, Ida.'

He lifted his head, his expression questioning. And something more. Something that made elation rise on gossamer wings.

You're imagining things. This is just physical for Cesare.

Yet the look in those dark, serious eyes made her heart judder.

When she managed to catch her breath, her voice was so husky it sounded unfamiliar. 'I feel the same.'

Later Ida couldn't remember crossing the foyer, checking in or getting to their suite.

All she recalled was the feel of Cesare's hand holding hers, the beating excitement in her chest and the glow in his eyes when the door closed behind them and they were finally alone.

Cesare's breathing was harsh in the stillness, the sound matching the heavy thrum of her pulse. Then she was in his arms, and he was striding towards the gilded, beautiful bedroom, his jaw clenched and an expression on his face that twisted her heart in her chest.

Awe, excitement and hope. She felt them all.

Ida was only human. She forgot about the world beyond Cesare's arms. The fact this was temporary. Instead, she listened to her eager heart.

CHAPTER FIFTEEN

Ida was in one of her favourite spots, on a trellis-shaded seat looking across the pool to the gardens and distant hills.

She tried to concentrate on the laptop Cesare had given her, but her mind drifted to their night in Florence.

Their fervour for each other had been even more potent than usual. They'd come together with an urgency that had blown her brain. Yet beneath the speed had been an emotion that made her heart swell.

Later, noting the crescent-shaped marks on Cesare's back where her nails had dug, and seeing the stubble rash of reddened skin on her breasts and belly, Ida had felt a curious mix of satisfaction and tenderness. Despite weeks of passionate encounters, nothing had felt as intimate as last night.

It wasn't just the sex. It was lying entwined on the vast bed, talking sleepily about everything and nothing. It was the laughter and sense of communion. The connection, as if some invisible thread bound them together.

Their intimacy had been about far more than she'd admitted. More than physical arousal. More than feeling safe with Cesare or grateful for his protection and the wonderful time they'd spent together.

In the early hours Cesare had held her to him and asked if she was happy. It hadn't occurred to Ida to be surprised by his question or cautious in responding, not with that sunburst of joy inside her. She'd told him the truth. That she'd never been happier.

For long moments they'd lain there, staring into each other's eyes.

Ida had no words for the feeling that had encompassed her then. Except maybe peace or belonging. Whatever it was, it had felt momentous. Neither had spoken, but finally Cesare had drawn her close and she'd nestled against him, head on his collarbone, their arms wrapped around each other as they fell asleep.

Cesare had brought her to the villa this morning but then turned to drive back to Florence, belatedly remembering a meeting he'd arranged. Ida had secretly been delighted, wondering if their time together was affecting him as well. She sat grinning, reliving every nuance of every word they'd shared.

Had she truly stumbled on a man who saw her for herself? Who really cared about her? Or did her own yearning blind her?

'*Signora.* A phone call for you.' Dorotea stepped through the open doorway, holding out a phone. 'A friend of yours.'

'*Grazie*, Dorotea.'

Ida took the phone. It could only be Jo, though why would her friend call the house instead of Ida's phone? 'Jo? How's it going?'

Silence crackled in her ear. Not the silence of Jo drawing breath but something else. Something that raised the hairs at her nape.

Ida sat straighter, senses alert.

Finally it came. But not the voice of any friend. It was the voice she'd told herself she'd never hear again.

'Hello, Ida,' he croaked. 'Enjoying your romantic tryst with Brunetti?'

She shot to her feet, her heart trying to burst free of her ribcage.

Her instinct was to throw the phone as far as she could, but fear and shock locked her fingers around it. Nausea rose so strong and fast she thought she'd vomit.

Ida swung towards the villa, opening her mouth as if to call back Dorotea.

'Don't even think about it,' her grandfather snarled, the faux gentleness of his first words obliterated by a familiar threatening tone. 'Call anyone and you'll regret it. You're being watched and I'll know if you disobey me.'

The clammy prickle at the back of Ida's neck spread across her whole body. She felt cold and hot at the same time as she turned to survey the garden and distant hills.

Was he here? Just outside the villa? Or one of his henchmen with a telephoto lens? A drone maybe?

Ida swallowed convulsively, her throat tight with terror at the thought of the old man watching her.

She opened her mouth to say something, but no sound came. It was stupid. All she had to do was call out and Dorotea would hear. Cesare's security team wouldn't let anyone on the premises without authority.

Yet logic was no match for fear, ingrained over years.

'That's better. I wouldn't like you doing something rash because there'd be consequences.'

He paused and Ida could hear his cruel smile.

'What do you want?'

'You wouldn't like anything to happen to Brunetti, would you?'

Dread was a blast of glacial air, shutting down her lungs and freezing her skin before seeping in to frost her bones. Ida's chest heaved as she struggled to breathe, her blood rushing in her ears.

At last, she found her voice. 'What are you saying?'

'He just left, didn't he? In that fast car of his, on these narrow roads. So easy to have an accident. A bit of gravel on the road, an unexpected oil slick on a curve. Or maybe a truck's brakes failing at the wrong moment.'

Ida could see it too clearly. Now her blood iced too.

She remembered the malevolence in her grandfather's eyes years before when he'd shoved her down the stairs, leaving her with concussion and a broken ankle. She thought of the people who'd died in the factory fire set on her grandfather's orders. Of the rumours of other crimes.

'I'm listening,' she said, her voice not her own.

'I thought you would be.' He laughed, the sound like bones rattling. 'You thought Brunetti would rescue you, didn't you? As if he'd ever care for a Calogero.'

I'm not a Calogero.

'Or is it the sex you like, you little slut?'

Fortunately something closed down inside Ida then. That same safety mechanism that had come to her rescue in the past when her grandfather started one of his diatribes. She heard the vile words but as if from a distance, so they didn't register. Just the violence behind them.

Ida found herself shaking, great, racking shudders of distress. If he harmed Cesare...

'What do you want?'

There was silence, as if her interruption surprised him.

'I want you here. *Now.* There's a car just beyond the gates. Walk down to it and let yourself out. You know the security code, I'm sure. If anyone asks, you're just going for a stroll.'

Ida shook her head. He really thought he could order her around any more?

'Don't defy me, girl!' His voice turned silky with threat. 'Unless you want your lover to pay. I can arrange it so he doesn't reach his office. Or maybe he'll get there and something unfortunate will happen. A gas explosion maybe.'

Ida's stomach churned with horror. Horror and a certainty her grandfather meant it. He never made empty threats.

She'd defied him by disappearing, ruining his plans. Meanwhile Cesare had somehow manoeuvred him out of the business and Fausto was being investigated by the police.

'Don't hurt him!'

A rusty chuckle filled her ear. 'Well, we'll have to see, won't we? Come to me and I promise he'll be safe for now. I have a new plan and you'll help me. You owe me.'

Ida swayed, bracing herself against the table.

'Don't go inside. Don't talk to anyone. Put the phone down and come to the gate.' He paused. 'If you're not here in seven minutes your lover will pay. That's a promise.'

The line went dead.

She snatched in a breath so sharp it felt as if she'd swallowed a razor. She lifted her head, but her eyes swam so much she couldn't make out anything but bright sunlight.

Ida jumped when the phone clattered onto the table.

She dragged in a breath, then another.

She couldn't go to her grandfather. She *couldn't*!

If she gave herself up to him, she'd never escape again. He'd use her in some new scheme and keep his claws in her for ever. *After* he'd meted out his vengeance for running away and spoiling his plans.

Ida felt hollow inside, except for the crushing weight pressing onto her chest.

Her one dream in all these years was to be free. Finally, after her marriage, she'd achieved that. Each day had felt glorious despite the drab routine of poverty and grinding, poorly paid work. Despite the fear that kept her in hiding.

So you weren't really free, were you? He was still dictating your life, even when he didn't know where you were. Because you lived in fear.

Ida rubbed a hand across aching eyes. She'd fought so hard for self-determination. How could she bear to give that up?

Because the alternative is to allow them to kill the man you love.

Ida slumped, boneless, against the table.

Strangely there was no shock at the revelation she loved Cesare.

It had been at the back of her consciousness for a while now. Even if it hadn't, a moment like this, of life-or-death danger, provided instant clarity.

After a lifetime learning not to trust men, especially wealthy, powerful men, she'd fallen for Cesare Brunetti heart and soul. It felt like the most natural thing in the world.

The most *wonderful* thing in the world. Cesare mightn't love her, but he'd rescued her from that sterile place where her soul had been locked. He'd brought her to life. He'd given her freedom and safety, joy, pleasure and a heady sense of hope.

The thought of him injured, dying...

Ida found herself walking on trembling legs into the garden. The rich scent of jasmine cloyed, turning rancid, as she imagined Cesare's car crumpled under a massive truck. Of his office blown apart by a bomb.

Her breath came in a gasping sob, and she slapped her palm over her mouth, lest Dorotea hear.

Ida forced back her shoulders and stepped onto the grass. With each pace her steps grew firmer.

She refused to allow the blackness that had shadowed her life to injure Cesare more than it had already.

She had no illusions. Fausto would punish her for what she'd done. She knew too that she took a gamble. There was no certainty he'd keep his word. Cesare could still be in danger.

But the alternative, to disobey, *knowing* Cesare would suffer...

Ida quickened her pace. It was a long way to the security gates. She couldn't be late.

'What do you mean, *gone*?'

Cesare scowled at the dark clouds closing in outside his window as he barked into the phone.

'She walked out,' Lorenzo explained. 'Dorotea said she took a call from a friend, a man. Ten minutes later she'd simply disappeared. Didn't even go back into the villa to get her purse.'

'A man? What man?'

None of this made sense. When Cesare had taken Ida back to the villa, she'd talked about relaxing for a while. He'd promised to be back late this afternoon and her slow smile had ratcheted up his libido. As if they hadn't spent last night sating a desire that seemed unquenchable.

'I'm pretty sure it was Fausto Calogero.'

'What?' Cesare's his eyes bulged. 'She'd never go back to him. Not after what he's done.' Cesare had witnessed her distress as she'd described life with Calogero and knew there was more she hadn't shared. His heart had gone out to her.

'Dorotea said it was an older man.'

'Even so—'

'I'm looking at the security film from the gate.'

'And?'

'She wasn't abducted. She typed the code into the keypad.'

Cesare's breath backed up in his lungs. Ida had left of her own volition? Without a word? There had to be more to this.

'She took a car from the garage?'

Maybe Ida was driving to the office, planning to surprise him. He imagined taking her out for a meal. Or locking the door and taking her on the desk.

That had to be it, she was coming here. The sultry look she'd given him earlier had been a clear promise.

'No, boss. She walked through the gates and got into a waiting car.' Lorenzo paused. 'I can send you the film, but I recognise the man. He works for Calogero. He's the one who was looking for her in London.'

Fear ghosted down Cesare's spine.

Bruno. Calogero's enforcer. The man who'd so terrified Ida that she'd leapt at the chance to fly to Tuscany, not even daring to collect her things.

'Send me the film.' He yanked his tie loose and strode to his desk, checking his computer. 'Did you follow them?'

'I didn't know she'd gone until it was too late. But I've got everyone onto it now. And I've put through a call to someone in the police. I hope to have news soon.'

Soon? That wasn't good enough.

But there was no point berating Lorenzo. His team's orders weren't to keep Ida prisoner.

Where had she gone? Above all, why leave with Bruno? Surely Lorenzo was wrong.

Cesare opened the security camera footage.

There was Ida, keying in the code to the gates. They swung wide and she stepped out, skirt fluttering around her legs. His heart hammered. It was the dress with velvet ribbons over her shoulders and beneath her breasts. She looked dainty and alluring, and she showed no hesitation as she walked, not once looking back.

She stopped. Her shoulders rose as if she took a deep breath. But she only paused a second before approaching a car with tinted windows. The door was open, held by a burly man with a wrestler's physique. Even from a distance Cesare recognised him. The smashed nose, thick neck and impassive face. Not impassive now. The way he looked at Ida churned nausea through Cesare's gut.

But she hadn't baulked.

Ida walked out of the safety of Cesare's home straight to the men she feared. Of her own free will. If Bruno was there, so was Calogero, in the car or waiting elsewhere.

Cesare's head spun.

There was no reason for Ida to do this. He could protect her from her grandfather. He *had* protected her. She was happy with Cesare. She'd told him so and he'd seen it for himself. The way she smiled more, the sound of her laughter, the joy in her eyes.

What had changed?

Maybe nothing had changed.

The insidious voice wove through his thoughts, but he refused to listen.

Cesare hit replay on the security film.

Apart from that instant's pause, when it looked as if Ida gathered herself, there was nothing to indicate hesitation about leaving with the man she'd so feared.

Maybe she hadn't feared him after all. Maybe they were allies, not enemies. Maybe she was playing a long game and you were a fool.

Cesare's breath turned to ash on his tongue.

It was impossible.

He knew the real Ida now. She'd never willingly associate with Calogero or his bruiser.

Again Cesare hit replay. Was that really a momentary pause, or was Ida drawing a breath of relief at being off his property?

Maybe she wanted to go back to her family.

Maybe Calogero wasn't her enemy.

Maybe she spun you lies.

Cesare scowled at the ridiculous idea. And at the searing pain ripping through his belly.

He only had her word for what she'd said about her history.

Maybe Calogero hadn't forced her into compliance.

Maybe she'd been a willing pupil. Learning to scheme and lie.

But Cesare had surprised her in London. She hadn't known he was looking for her.

Unless Calogero's staff had you under surveillance and briefed Ida.

Unless she set you up.

His heart dived. Yet what would she gain? An affair with him wouldn't stop their divorce and she'd signed the papers. The prenup was watertight.

Another scandal? The missing wife returns then

disappears again? Cesare frowned. After what he'd already weathered, a bit more gossip meant nothing.

What had she and Calogero to gain?

Ida had been in the villa. She'd had the run of the place, including when he wasn't there. Yet no valuables had gone missing. Ida wasn't a thief.

Cesare's breath fractured and clawing talons scored his windpipe. She'd used his study, often curling up on a sofa there, using the laptop he'd given her. He knew she'd been investigating interior-design courses. Had she been investigating something else too?

Had she hacked into his computer?

He'd broken Calogero's death grip on the company and the old man was about to go down for a range of crimes. But wasn't a cornered animal all the more dangerous?

Had Calogero sent Ida to gather information about the investigations into his crimes, and to locate remaining weaknesses in the Brunetti company?

Cesare turned his back on the screen. He couldn't watch the footage any more.

His heart told him Ida was genuine. That she wasn't a schemer. That she hadn't betrayed him. Yet cold, unemotional logic gave a different perspective.

Cesare had learned in childhood how foolish men could be when in thrall to a beautiful woman. Ida wasn't merely beautiful. She was fascinating, enticing and passionate. She made his blood pump faster and the world seem brighter.

He snatched a breath that didn't fill his cramped lungs.

Had he inherited his father's weakness?

Had he let his libido undermine caution? Had he allowed himself to fall under the spell of a woman who used him to get what she wanted?

Cesare's nape tightened and sweat beaded his brow.

He'd crossed every boundary his *nonno* had taught him. He'd been impulsive. He'd confused business with pleasure, giving emotions free rein. Trusting without demanding proof. His honourable instinct to protect a vulnerable woman had morphed into something more profound and potentially self-destructive.

Had he made the biggest mistake of his life?

CHAPTER SIXTEEN

IDA WOKE HORRIBLY. A headache beat through her skull in time with her hammering pulse and there was something wrong with her mouth.

She lifted her hand to investigate but found something wrong with that too. It took long, befuddled seconds to realise there was something wrapped around her wrists, tying them together. And something around her mouth as well. Panicked, she tried to swallow over the musty taste in her mouth and realised her mouth was filled with fabric, held in place by a gag.

Her eyes snapped open, and she immediately closed them as pain spiked. Cautiously she squinted against the light, inhaling through her nose, fighting rising panic.

Slowly things began to make sense. She lay on her side on a marble floor, its chill leaching into her body. She was in a large sitting room, sombrely and expensively decorated in the style of several centuries ago. She saw gilded antique furniture, dark paintings and heavy velvet curtains partly drawn across tall windows.

Memory surfaced.

Bruno had brought her to this place, a venerable mansion where her grandfather had been waiting.

Convulsively Ida swallowed, fear rising anew as

she recalled the scene. Her grandfather had looked far older and more fragile than she remembered. So bad that she'd wondered if he was ill. But his temper hadn't changed.

There'd been sneering triumph and malevolent anticipation in his face as he'd derided her for thinking she could escape him.

He had a use for her, he'd said. First to make Cesare suffer and then as a bargaining chip to get Cesare to call off his investigators. If that didn't work... His voice had turned soft, and Ida's skin had crawled. That was when her grandfather was most dangerous.

He'd peppered her with questions about Cesare, his business and plans. As if Ida would betray Cesare to him!

She'd pleaded ignorance again and again, but that had only infuriated Calogero. For the first time she saw him spooked, fear crossing his jaundiced features as he spoke of someone prying into his affairs. Someone who'd outmanoeuvred his own security.

A flicker of hope had flared. Her grandfather thought it was just Cesare pursuing him. He didn't realise it was the police across several countries. Maybe they were close to an arrest? Cesare had thought so.

Finally, her grandfather's temper had peaked and he'd lashed out, knocking her off her feet. She'd taken a step to save herself but caught her foot in the edge of a carpet and lost her balance.

That explained the pounding skull. It must have connected with the stone floor. Gingerly she lifted her tied hands and discovered a lump on her head. Nausea filled her at that gentle probing, and she had to stop and rest.

While she'd been unconscious someone, Bruno, no doubt, had bound and gagged her. Why? Her grandfather would have people here who'd stop her leaving.

Ida forced herself to lie still and think.

Did she hear voices? Or was it the sound of her pulse?

She scrabbled at the gag but only the tips of her fingers were free of their binding and she couldn't get enough purchase.

Ignoring the screaming pain, she rolled forward, bracing her joined hands and getting onto her knees. Her head swam but she fought it. When her head cleared she was sure of it, there were voices near by. Masculine voices.

Her heart leapt. Was she crazy to imagine that deep tone was Cesare's?

Looking for something to help her up, for her feet were tied too, Ida discovered a spindly-legged sofa and side table beside her. On the table was a glass, a fine goblet with the look of age.

Teetering on her knees, Ida lifted the goblet clumsily in her bound hands. She shot a look towards the door. It was still closed, the voices muffled.

Silently she prayed it wasn't Bruno talking with

her grandfather but someone who might help her escape. She had to warn Cesare he was in danger.

'You always were stubborn, Brunetti, just like your grandfather.' Calogero shook his head. 'Why would I kidnap your wife? You can't blame me if she wasn't happy with you.' His eyes flashed maliciously. 'You made a spectacle of yourself driving her away the first time. But to do it twice? You've made yourself a laughing stock.'

His croaky chuckle was like poison dripping on unprotected flesh.

Cesare's skin crawled. Beneath his veneer of calm, he'd never known such violent emotion. It was hard thinking beyond the haze of fury at this man.

'But if she does seek sanctuary here,' the old devil continued, 'in the bosom of her family, I'll take her in and shelter her. If you've maltreated her...'

Cesare stood unmoving, refusing to react to such slander. He wasn't the one who'd treated Ida badly.

He glanced at the stocky man standing in a corner behind where Calogero sat at his oversized desk. Bruno looked every inch the thug Ida had described him. The thought of her at that man's mercy carved a hollow through Cesare's belly.

'Yet Ida was seen leaving my villa with your man.' He nodded at Bruno.

'You astound me.' Calogero swung around in his seat. 'What do you know about this, Bruno?'

'Nothing, boss.' He turned his blank gaze to Cesare. 'Whoever saw it was mistaken. I haven't seen her in years.'

The curl at the corners of his mouth belied his words.

Cesare itched to force the truth from his lying mouth. It might yet come to that, but Cesare suspected violence wouldn't get him far. Calogero would call in reinforcements and Cesare would be overpowered before he could find her.

Frustration rose, but behind it was fear that he was too late. The desperate urge to smash through this pretence vied with cold dread. But revealing his feelings would be disastrous.

Calogero was a vampire, living off others, sucking them dry in his quest for power, riches and recognition.

'Well,' Cesare murmured, flexing constricted shoulders. 'That's unfortunate. I had a proposition for you but if you don't know where she is...' He spread his hands, palms up. 'Never mind. I won't waste any more of your time.'

'What proposition?'

Calogero might be a devious strategist and downright dangerous, but he'd never make a poker player. Those rheumy eyes glistened greedily, and he sat forward, knobbly hands spread on the desk, practically slavering in anticipation.

Cesare met his eyes but didn't speak straight away.

'You want to punish her, don't you? That's why

you want her so badly,' the creaky voice continued, and to Cesare's disgust the old man smiled approvingly. 'I can't blame you. A man isn't a man if he can't control his womenfolk.'

Cesare bit back a riposte that a *real* man didn't need to control anyone. But he wasn't here to argue. The stakes were too high.

'Since you have no idea where she is, there's no point discussing it. If she contacts you, call me and we can do business.'

He swung around as if to leave, his heart pummelling his ribcage. If this didn't work…

'Perhaps… Who knows? Maybe I can help you after all. What are you offering?'

Slowly Cesare turned back. Then he drew out the paper his lawyer had drawn up under strenuous protest in the time it had taken Cesare to drive to the address Lorenzo had found.

Calogero sat forward, his spidery body ready to pounce.

Cesare tossed the paper onto the desk and watched him grab it, eyes widening as he read. Then read again. Finally, he sat back. 'This is nothing. Not a contract, just a memorandum of understanding. It's not binding.'

'It will carry weight in a court of law if we both sign it.' Cesare paused, letting that sink in. 'Or if you prefer to wait…' He glanced at his watch, wondering how long before the others arrived. 'My legal team is drawing up the detailed contract now. I didn't give them much time, but I wanted to prove my intentions in the meantime.'

The old man said nothing. Cesare could see the wheels turning in his brain.

'But it's academic,' Cesare continued. 'The offer stands only if Ida is returned to me. Immediately. Since you don't know her whereabouts...'

Yellowed teeth were bared in a smile that was as eager as it was horrible. 'There may be a way I could help. As a favour to an old friend.'

Cesare checked a contemptuous sneer, merely raising his eyebrows. 'Go on.'

'If I were to find the girl and bring her to you—'

'Not good enough. I want her *now*.'

He drew a fountain pen from his pocket and approached the desk. Calogero licked his lips and looked down at the paper. The man was greedy. He wanted the deal, but he wanted to keep Ida too.

Every muscle in Cesare's body drew taut as he forced himself to hold back.

But it was no good, the need to find Ida was overwhelming. He leaned across the desk, reaching for his nemesis, when a thud made him turn. A door to his left slammed against the wall.

'Ida!'

She was pale, the bright, dishevelled hair tumbling around her shoulders contrasting with her stark pallor. And the bright red stains on her hands.

Cesare's heart plummeted as anger combusted into incandescent rage. What had they done to her?

'Don't sign it!' she gasped. 'Don't give him any-thing.'

Cesare got to her in a few strides, but Bruno had reached her first. He'd been standing in that corner. He grabbed Ida by the shoulders, shoving her back towards the door.

Cesare acted instinctively. Later he could only re-call the feel of a hard muscled shoulder beneath his hand as he swung the bodyguard around. Bruno's massive fist hurtling towards his face. The blocking movement he'd learned all those years ago work-ing in the slums. The sound of bone crunching as Cesare's heel connected with Bruno's knee. And the impact of his knuckles on solid flesh, both fists in quick succession, followed by the gasp of the winded man and the thud as he toppled to the floor.

Then Ida was in Cesare's arms.

He ran his hands over her, checking for more inju-ries, eyes widening at the bright blood welling from her hands. There were shallow cuts between her fin-gers and at her wrists. The sight woke a growling beast inside him.

'What did they do to you?'

His throat was so tight he barely got the words out.

Ida buried her face in his chest, hands clenching on his shirt, and he swore his heart stopped. 'You're here! You're really here.'

'Shh, it's all right, Ida.'

He couldn't believe she was safe in his arms. The

last couple of hours felt like an eternity in which he'd aged decades. Relief was so sharp it cut his very soul, severing something within that had been bound tight and hard.

In his peripheral vision Cesare saw movement. The old man lifting a phone to his ear, gabbling about help.

Holding Ida close, Cesare crossed to the desk, plucked the phone from Calogero and threw it across the room. It shattered against inlaid marble.

Cesare's breath came as short punches of oxygen.

'You wouldn't harm an old man!'

Cesare surveyed him, cowering in his seat. He wanted to smash Calogero. To make him pay.

Instead, he drew a deep, scouring breath and fought for restraint. His arms settled around Ida, cradling her close, her soft body like a benediction, a lightness in the dark whirlpool of his rage.

Calogero would pay. But Cesare would not lower himself to the villain's standards.

Holding the old man's gaze, he reached for the agreement, crumpled it slowly in his fist and shoved it in his pocket. Then he lifted Ida into his arms and marched to the door. 'It's okay, *cara*. It's over.'

There it was, the sound of sirens and pounding on the street door. The police had been almost ready to haul Calogero in for questioning. Cesare's urgent call had brought that forward.

He took the staircase slowly, conscious of his precious burden.

On the ground floor a number of heavy-set men in suits appeared but didn't try to stop him. Not with police demanding entry. Calogero's thugs were wondering about their future.

Cesare strode through the now open door and didn't look back.

He'd been kindness itself, holding her until the shaking stopped. Sitting with her in the ambulance while a medic checked the bump on her head, gave her a painkiller and saw to the shallow cuts she'd got while sawing through her bonds with broken glass.

Cesare had been everything she could wish for. He'd rescued her when she feared she might never escape. The sound of his voice, the sight of him as she staggered into the room, had almost undone her. He'd dealt with her grandfather and Bruno, the men she'd lived in fear of for so long. He'd even brushed past the police, insisting they wait to question her. Then he'd taken her to his villa, draping his jacket over her shivering shoulders.

Ida should be ecstatic. Instead she felt sick.

For he'd barely spoken. He avoided her eyes as if he couldn't bear to look at her.

She hadn't heard everything her grandfather had said. But Cesare must know she'd chosen to go there.

Did he think she'd thrown in her lot with her grandfather, who'd later turned against her for reasons of his own?

She knew a deep vein of mistrust ran through

Cesare. Mistrust of the Calogero family. And of women. She'd heard Cesare's contempt, not just for his father, who he deemed weak, but also for the women he believed had seduced his father.

Did he see her as another mercenary woman out to get what she could? Just as he had when they first met?

The time they'd shared here had been golden with promise and burgeoning love. *For her.*

But for Cesare? Sometimes it had felt as if they hovered on the brink of something wonderful. She'd been almost certain Cesare was opening his heart to her, but he'd never said so.

Perhaps she'd imagined that. Certainly he wasn't loverlike now. He kept his distance and wouldn't meet her eyes.

She'd misinterpreted his passion for the beginnings of love. Though he'd made it clear this was a temporary arrangement.

They were getting divorced! How could she have imagined he felt more?

Ida blinked prickling eyes and turned away from the silent man on the sofa opposite. Night had fallen and outside the underwater lights turned the pool into a shimmering oasis. It was almost too beautiful. She couldn't bear this any more.

She drained her glass of water and made to rise.

'Ida, we need to talk.'

Her head snapped around. Cesare's expression

hadn't altered. He still looked as communicative as a statue, his big frame rigid.

She shuddered beneath the silk-lined warmth of his jacket. 'I'm sorry,' she blurted out. 'I did what I had to.'

Her throat closed as she remembered the threat to harm Cesare. Ridiculous that it still upset her now he was safe, yet hot tears flooded her eyes.

'Ida, don't. Please.' His voice was harsh but a beautiful sort of harsh, almost tender. It made the tears come faster because she must be imagining the tenderness. To her dismay he rose and sat beside her.

She groped for a tissue, plunging her hand into the jacket pocket, fingers closing around crumpled paper.

Ida sniffed and withdrew it, bending her head as if fascinated by the paper instead of the man beside her.

A handkerchief appeared before her and she took it with a nod of thanks, dabbing at her eyes. 'Sorry. It's just reaction.'

'Don't apologise.' His voice was harsh. 'I was wrong. You should have a good cry if it makes you feel better.'

But Ida didn't want to weep. She wanted to end this torture, sitting with the man she loved, knowing it was all over. It was obvious he didn't return her feelings. If he thought she'd been in league with her grandfather, he probably despised her.

He'd saved her because he was a decent man. He'd have done the same for anyone.

Ida turned towards him but didn't meet his eyes. 'Did I thank you? I can't remember. It's a bit of a blur.' *Liar.* Today's events were branded on her brain. 'But I appreciate all you've done. And don't worry, as soon as the police have finished with their questions, I'll go.'

Her nervous babble died when a warm hand covered her bare arm. 'I'm sorry, Ida. You must have been terrified.'

'You've got nothing to be sorry for.'

Unthinking, she met Cesare's eyes and then couldn't look away. His expression matched how she felt. Anguished.

She blinked. It couldn't be.

'If you'd felt safe here you wouldn't have gone to him. If you'd believed in me.'

Cesare's mouth compressed to a thin line and Ida saw that flicker of pulse at his temple, something she'd seen in moments of extreme emotion. She stared at his drawn features. Was it possible he felt *guilty*?

She shifted and instantly his hand dropped.

'*You're* not responsible, Cesare.'

'No?' His lips curled. 'If you felt you could trust me, you'd have come to me instead of going to him when he demanded it. I thought you *knew* I'd protect you. Hadn't I made that clear?'

He didn't wait for an answer. 'It's my fault you

don't trust me. It's because of how I treated you before, isn't it? Because of my prejudice.' He yanked his tie lower, dragging his collar undone as if it were too tight. 'I failed you.'

Agog, Ida digested Cesare's words. He wasn't berating her for being in league with her grandfather. He blamed himself for her leaving!

'What hold did he have over you, Ida? How did he force you to go without even telling me?'

Ida stared, still unable to believe what she'd heard. When she spoke her voice seemed to come from far away. 'You don't think I was working with him?'

Cesare's head jerked back. 'Working with him? You were terrified of him.'

Ida's heart galloped and she felt light-headed. She licked suddenly dry lips. 'You believe I was a victim?'

He looked down at the bandages on her hands, his expression truly ferocious. 'Believe? I know it.' Then his eyes held hers, his gaze searching. 'What did he threaten, Ida? How did he get you there?'

It was so unexpected, to have this powerful man who'd once lived and breathed mistrust, believing her without question. As if their early history and his prejudices meant nothing.

Because he believes in you.

Could it be true?

A squall of emotions tumbled through her. Amazement, joy and disbelief so strong she felt like crying and laughing at once. Her shoulders shook but her eyes were dry and staring.

Now she saw something in his dark gaze that hijacked the breath from her lungs. Something strong and tender. Something like the yearning she felt.

Cesare's hands were gentle on her upper arms. 'You're safe now. He can't hurt you, truly. With the evidence against him across two countries there's no way he'll be bailed. I suspect he'll spend the rest of his life behind bars.'

Ida swallowed, trying to find words as her heart swelled. 'Cesare.' It was a whisper, barely louder than her pulse, and he leaned closer. 'You...trust me?'

For so long she'd been entangled in a world of duplicity and sham, of threats, fear and mistrust. She'd told herself again and again that Cesare's attentions were the fleeting product of lust. But this felt *real*.

'Absolutely.' He lifted one bandaged hand and carefully pressed his lips to a patch of bare skin. 'When I heard you'd gone I died a thousand deaths, imagining what might happen to you.'

Ida hung on his words yet still couldn't quite take them in. Almost as if she wanted him to recant and admit he'd doubted her. 'But I wasn't kidnapped. I walked straight out.'

'I saw the film and it almost broke my heart.' Another kiss to her fingers, more fervent than the last, sending a shaft of heat through her chilled body.

'Everything I'd learned about manipulation told me you'd played me for a fool.'

His hand tightened as she made to draw back. 'But my heart knew better. It told me the only way you'd go to him was because you'd been forced. What was it? Did he threaten your cousin in Scotland?'

Ida looked into that proud, concerned, dear face and wondered how she'd doubted him. What she saw there overwhelmed her. This time when she blinked back tears, they were tears of joy.

'It's okay. We can talk later. You need rest.'

'No! What I need is you, Cesare. Only you.' She turned her hand to grip his and lift it to her mouth, inhaling that unique scent of cedar, citrus and hot, delectable male that she'd become addicted to. She kissed his hand, tasting the salty essence of him.

Long fingers threaded through her hair, gently massaging her scalp and drawing her closer. She wanted to sink against him but he was right. They needed to talk.

'He threatened to harm you. Either a car accident on the drive into Florence or an explosion at the office.' Ida felt Cesare stiffen. 'He told me I was being watched and that if I made an attempt to talk to anyone, or send a message, you'd pay. I believed him.'

Silence but for Cesare's ragged breathing. Finally he spoke, his voice hoarse. 'You walked into danger for *my* sake?'

She lifted her shoulders. 'I couldn't bear the thought of him harming you.'

Cesare drew their joined hands against his wide chest, so she felt his drumming heart. 'You're the bravest woman I know.'

Ida shook her head. 'Not brave. Just desperate.'

Heat flared in that liquid dark gaze, tugging at her heart.

'I knew you were remarkable,' he murmured. 'Right from the beginning there was something about you that made me weak for you. But I never guessed the half of how amazing you are.' His expression was full of admiration and something so powerfully tender that Ida's soul soared. 'I don't understand what I've done to deserve such incredible loyalty. Such sacrifice.'

To Ida's amazement Cesare's deep voice wobbled on the last word before his jaw clamped tight.

'After what you've done for me? You gave me hope in dark times. You gave me...'

Her words faded as she struggled to explain how he'd turned her life around, giving her not merely security but happiness such as she'd never known and a renewed determination not simply to hide from her grandfather, but also to build a positive future.

'I didn't give anything you didn't deserve.' Still holding her hand to his chest, Cesare skimmed his knuckles along her cheek and a seam of longing opened up in her heart. 'Even when we married and I told myself it was just sexual desire I felt, I *knew* you were important to me, Ida. Maybe that's why I reacted so badly. I didn't want to be vulnerable.'

Cesare grimaced. 'Learning the truth, learning about *you*, has made me question everything I was so sure I knew. The old mantra of duty over passion, strategy and success instead of love, none of that worked any more.'

His palm cupped her face. 'You mean so much to me. I love you, Ida.'

Shock made her stiffen and instantly Cesare released her, his mouth flattening.

'It's too early, I know. I shouldn't have blurted that out. Blame it on shock.' In one swift movement he was on his feet, stalking away then spinning on his heel to look back at her, his chest expanding on a huge breath. 'I only realised what this feeling was today, when I thought I'd lost you. But you've had enough for now. This can wait.'

'No, it can't!' Ida didn't feel tired now. There was enough energy sparking through her to light up a whole city. 'I just wasn't expecting—'

'I know it's hard to believe after the way I behaved. I've got a lot of catching up to do.'

He was flagellating himself over the past when none of that mattered. Ida's hands curled in her lap and something crackled. She glanced down to see a paper on her lap, smoothed flat by her restless hands.

And then she didn't hear anything else Cesare said.

There was a roaring in her ears like a high-speed train and she shook all over as if from its vibration.

'Cesare?' Her voice when it came was thin and high. 'You were going to do this? For me?' When she lifted her head, she looked into eyes so intent she felt his stare as a tangible, stroking caress. 'You were going to give him a controlling share of Brunetti Enterprises?'

Even reading the words in black and white, it seemed impossible.

'If it meant getting you back.'

'Cesare, you couldn't! It's your family firm. The thing you worked for and loved all your life. It's tradition and history and family.'

Ida knew those were as vital to him as the blood flowing in his veins. His pride in his family's achievements, his concern for those dependent on the company and his focus on innovation and success were part of him.

Yet he didn't say it had been a ploy to trick her grandfather. Instead, a slow smile edged the corners of his mouth. Not a confident grin. For remarkably, Cesare looked anything but self-assured.

'I've found something I love more.'

Ida's hand went to her throat where her heart thrashed as if trying to escape.

'I still want what's best for the company. I'll still do all I can to protect it and nurture it, but I've learned that a business is just that. It's not my life and I don't want it to be. Given a choice between saving you and the company, it had to be you.'

He went on, seemingly oblivious to her shock. 'Even after you signed the divorce papers I couldn't bring myself to give them to my lawyer. They're sitting in my desk drawer.' He read her stunned expression and nodded. 'Yes, even then, *tesoro*. Though I didn't understand why. I just knew I suddenly wasn't ready to end our marriage and I needed to know why.'

Cesare paced towards her and with every step the glow in his eyes dissolved the last vestiges of doubt. 'My priorities have shifted. I'd rather have love.' His voice was whisky and gravel and utterly compelling because she heard the raw ache there. It matched the sweet shaft of pleasure-pain inside her. Again Ida saw that vein throb at his temple. 'If you give me a chance. With time…'

Remarkably Cesare seemed to run out of steam, as if the persuasive words he'd once wielded so easily were now beyond him. He lifted his shoulders and spread his hands as if inviting her to take a chance on him.

Inviting.

Not demanding.

Not cornering her so she had no choice.

Not putting his desires above her own.

Once Ida had thought him similar to her grandfather, ruthless and self-focused. She'd been wrong.

Cesare looked almost as vulnerable as she felt.

Ida felt the flutter of paper against her leg as she rose, eyes locked on Cesare's.

'You trust me.' Her voice was a wisp of air. 'You care for me.' Her words were firmer now. 'You make me feel worthy of love.' Something she hadn't experienced for so long. 'I can't tell you how much that means.'

'You don't need to explain, Ida. You make me feel the same.'

'I've never in my life felt as good as I do with you, Cesare.' There, she'd admitted it, the truth she'd shied from for weeks. 'Because I love you too. I've loved you such a long time, even when I tried not to.'

Suddenly his arms were around her, tender but firm. Those dark eyes that looked to Ida like paradise gleamed overbright. The smile curling the corners of his mouth made her heart want to fly.

'Does that mean you'll take a chance with me, Ida?'

She shook her head. 'It's not taking a chance, my love.' How wonderful it felt to say those words. 'I believe in you. I believe in *us*. I've never been more certain of anything as I am that we're meant for each other.'

Cesare smiled down at her, letting all he felt show. Then, because words were superfluous, he drew her close and proved in other ways exactly how precious she was to him.

EPILOGUE

'Have I told you how gorgeous you look, *tesoro*?'

In the full-length mirror Ida saw Cesare approach, looking too scrumptious and tempting for a woman expecting a houseful of guests in a few minutes. She'd like to drag that formal black jacket from his wide shoulders, tug the silk bow tie undone and have her wicked way with him.

From Cesare's smug expression he read her thoughts. Not surprising, since they were so attuned.

'You've mentioned it once or twice.' She grinned as he stopped behind her. 'But I don't object to repetition.'

He bent and kissed that sensitive spot at the base of her neck that made her skin tingle and butterflies swarm deep inside.

'That dress looks magnificent on you.' His teeth skimmed her flesh and she shuddered as delicious sensations shot through her. 'But you look wonderful no matter how you dress. Or even if you don't dress.' Cesare made a sound at the back of his throat, a soft, purring growl of approval that liquefied her knees. '*Especially* if you don't dress.'

Ida leaned back against her husband, letting him take her weight.

In the mirror she saw a woman in a form-fitting lace dress of seafoam-green that matched her eyes. A woman wearing such a look of such dazed delight

Ida knew she needed time to make herself presentable before their guests arrived.

But then Cesare met her gaze in the mirror, sliding his arms around her to rest his broad palms on the tiny swell of her abdomen, and suddenly Ida didn't care about the guests. Not the renowned interior designer who'd just offered Ida a part-time job. Or even Kate and Jo, who'd flown in for the anniversary party, arriving on the same flight as Francesco, who was driving them here to the villa now.

'Happy?' Ida asked, her voice husky.

'It's impossible to explain how much.' He stroked his hand over the spot where their first child nestled. 'You changed my whole life, Ida. You know that, don't you?'

'You changed mine too.' And she didn't just mean because her grandfather and his thugs were behind bars. 'Sometimes I can't believe how lucky I am.'

'It's more than luck, my love. You deserve all the happiness in the world.'

'So do you. You're the best man I know.'

The world blurred as Cesare spun her around and drew her tight against him, his head lowering.

'I've just put on my lipstick!'

Too late. His mouth was on hers in a kiss so full of love and just-controlled passion that Ida didn't even try to resist.

Finally, Cesare lifted his head and frowned. 'I hear a car.' He sighed. 'You've just got time to refresh your lipstick.'

Ida breathed deep, inhaling the familiar scent of this man she adored.

'Some things are more important than lipstick. I've decided on a more natural look for tonight. Besides, Dorotea will answer the door and take their coats.'

'Which gives us another few minutes.'

He pulled her to him, and Ida laughed with pure delight.

Her instinct when they'd met all those years ago had proved correct. Marriage to Cesare Brunetti was everything she'd hoped for and so much more.

* * * * *

If you fell in love with
Reclaiming His Runaway Cinderella,
Annie West's 50th book for Harlequin Presents,
you're sure to adore these other stories
by the author!

A Consequence Made in Greece
The Innocent's Protector in Paradise
Claiming His Virgin Princess
One Night with Her Forgotten Husband
The Desert King Meets His Match

Available now!